# SPLANX

# SPLANX

Peter Magliocco

COSMIC
EGG
BOOKS

Winchester, UK
Washington, USA

First published by Cosmic Egg Books, 2014
Cosmic Egg Books is an imprint of John Hunt Publishing Ltd., Laurel House, Station Approach,
Alresford, Hants, SO24 9JH, UK
office1@jhpbooks.net
www.johnhuntpublishing.com

For distributor details and how to order please visit the 'Ordering' section on our website.

ISBN: 978 1 78279 498 1

A CIP catalogue record for this book is available from the British Library.

Design: Stuart Davies

Printed in the USA by Edwards Brothers Malloy

We operate a distinctive and ethical publishing philosophy in all
areas of our business, from our global network of authors to
production and worldwide distribution.

*It is probably true that there is no single language that can express the many levels of consciousness through which it is possible to perceive the totality of phenomena and entities.*

– from *Joseph Beuys* by Caroline Tisdall

*To use the body as a means of expressing the anguish of the human soul is no longer a possible enterprise; we do not know how to represent the body and do not believe in the existence of the soul.*

– from *The Romantic Rebellion,* by Kenneth Clark

# Part I

The Paranormal Eye

# Chapter I

# In The Prismatic Window's Killing Dream

It was no dream, it was no nightmare. It was like a paranormal vision of something he was forced to see, one of many he was used to seeing as a paranormal investigator, of course, and Resi had little choice but to obey. It was his job, he kept telling himself. Ease through the tremors of any ghostly assault. Her screaming inside the distant room was probably not heard by others, only himself. He heard too clearly, and all the Dutch beer from the downstairs bar wouldn't stop it.

"Help me...please!" the voice kept wailing. Her voice – Laira's – was invading a vast section of an energized space. She had been so recently a part of the place, yet now she was evanescent energy in a shifting geography of time and space. Resi might as well have been in that room instead of his closet-like own; the wailing kept penetrating the aged paper thin walls. In the dark his hypersensitive eyes squeezed shut almost automatically with each wail. He was an instrument being played upon.

"Stop him...please stop him!"

*Damn it,* Carlton Resi said to himself.

He sat up suddenly, wanting to scream himself. His own nervous system's spasm was distinct enough, churning words through interior alerts, and in disgust he ripped off his tungsten ear piece. A gift of an ex-CEO of Paranormal Entity, when he was just starting out...He sat there on the small bed staring at its funny quilted spread. When the tremors gradually diminished inside him, he realized a silence broken only by his own labored breathing remained. The voice's screaming had stopped, and his body had not imploded totally yet.

He looked at his luminous watch. It was only a little past 11 o'clock.

He had to get out of the hotel, he had to get going. It didn't matter, as long as he followed his game plan. Once again he booted up his silver computer to check his notes. It glowed as a supercilious part of his own being for reasons he couldn't fathom. The ghost in his machine was something he relied on for his work, but this was different; each time he felt the definite emanation of something subtly invading his vision. Affecting him in its digitally subversive manner, as if he were connected to another operating system, making him sick, weary, hypertensive, when just a few days ago he'd been anything but.

It was only his third night in Amsterdam, working for the Magister and already things were a jumble. Facts were becoming fictions. He had to hold on, skip the booze no matter what, no matter how much the tremors were threatening to overcome him. He retrieved his super Cyplex international cell phone, an exclusive and expensive part of his investigative arsenal. Already he'd taken several thermal photos of the Hotel Nieuw from a cigarette-burned end table and tried once more to reach his office in Los Angeles, but only got robotic voice mail. Angrily he stubbed out another cigarette and cursed. For a few more days he must hold on, then maybe he could get on top of this thing. But the computer codes reflecting pixels from his eyes meant otherwise.

Outside in the hallway he slowly navigated his way on the second floor towards the room he felt the energy still extruding from. It had beckoned to Resi his first night in the hotel and he'd made the mistake of entering it himself, not the paranormal eye. Now he was ready for it again. Its faint odor of plum trees suggested pleasant summer fragrances despite the overcast late fall weather outside. He took out his EMF device for measuring spiritual energy and glanced at the dancing numbers as he approached Laira McKinney's room, or what had once been hers. He stopped before the large door with its gold and cursive numeral '7' almost shimmering before his eyes. Hearing something like moaning coming from within, he quietly knocked on the scratched purple wood and felt a weird heat there. *What the fuck,* Resi asked himself, watching the device's meter spike like crazy. He tried the locked door handle, another antiquated one, not round, something from the 19th century. No one could possibly be in there, not the missing young Laira at any rate. He knocked again, feeling his adrenalin kick in. The room was probably stone empty, it had to be after the event he'd just heard, but the door slowly opened to reveal a boy with a frizzy red shock of hair, hardly a ten-year-old, who silently looked back out with an unfazed and stoic demeanor.

"Hi, I'm one of your neighbors…I heard some ruckus going on, is everything all right?"

The pale boy continued staring back with his hand still gripping the door handle. There didn't seem to be anyone else inside, certainly not of the adult variety, Resi noted, peering as much as possible into the room's dimness without actually eavesdropping. He realized the boy thought him odd-looking probably, standing there with the detector in his hand.

The pleasant room smell had given way to something decidedly unpleasant. It was an increasingly foul body odor smell, not coming from the boy, which had Resi even more perplexed. What he saw looked normal enough, he even caught a glimpse of the bed which was unruffled and bore no human presence, though a faint indentation still present suggested there recently had been. But whose was it? Slowly without saying a word the boy shut the door on Resi, who continued standing there, mouth half-open, now feeling like a peddler of some unwanted wares. He could feel something behind the door, some force of ectoplasm more disturbing than before, and Resi knocked again violently on the door.

"Laira? Are you okay…? *Laira!* It's Carlton Resi…!"

He saw an image which had flashed by on his computer

screen earlier, when he was in his own room, the image of a young woman's screaming face caught between a vise of smoky swirls and psychedelic colors now implanted on the faded purple door's canvas. A face he knew was Laira's became her severed head dancing bloodily before him, and Resi fell backwards, shouting out in surprise. Vectors of an uncharted cyber-world became invasive reality, scathing the air with warning.

Resi regained his balance and backed away, retrieving his dropped detector in the process. That was her room all right, and the boy its guardian.

Downstairs he passed the reception desk and placed his key, attached to a large and toy-like wooden top, into the drop. He was back in an archaic and befuddling world, one where his hi-tech devices were frowned on and paranormal gum shoes laughed at. So be it. He could hear the TV in an adjacent bar and saw part of the young clerk in profile, watching it. There was little heat in the vicinity and a penetrating chill prevailed. Resi's nervous system wasn't taking it well, despite the heavy leather jacket and gloves he wore. The bored clerk was pulling another night shift, uninterested and annoyed by a few of the questions Resi now suddenly asked him.

"Could you please tell me the guest's name in number seven? I'm wondering if it might be a friend of mine I'm expecting."

No one was in that unit, the clerk testily replied. It had yet to be booked.

"Are you sure?"

Resi could hear the disappointment in his own voice as he thanked the clerk anyway.

Now he opened the creaking, frosty-glassed door dividing the hallway from the other doors. The babble of the TV faded into white noise as he went through the foyer and into the unpleasant street coldness. He was in a time warp. He was in the same city but it might well be over ten years before, when he was an American student at this same hotel, a few decades old but already standing. (Young, when you thought about it, compared to the other city buildings.) Some force jolted his memory back to that point, when he'd first met the poet Laira McKinney at a café reading. He had thoroughly enjoyed talking with her, gaining some insight into the craft a beautifully attractive young girl like her, still a teenager, practiced with such noteworthy success. Yet remembering it, Resi wasn't feeling like a young thirty-five-year-old at all, and he was destined to get much older very quickly if he didn't confront her presence again in the strange room whose door he had opened to a ghostly world.

*Don't tell anyone why you're here.* He had told himself this the night of his arrival in Amsterdam, when he'd begun to be queasy and disoriented. The secret about why he was here, Resi intended to keep, like some personal taboo, from anyone unnecessarily prying. Only he would know it fully.

Resi could not tell anyone but his mini-staff back in the states what had been happening to him: The fact that one night an imperfect knowledge, more an intuition really, had simmered in his head and taken shape, substance and form within his mechanized dreams into the entity of one young woman; Laira, who he knew briefly from that earlier time in Europe and was supposedly now dead. At least in the flesh…? When the Magister had called him for this job it was the start of resuming a prophetic destiny, Resi believed.

And his computer had verified it.

Of course 'The Paranormal Eye,' as many called him, was generally in good health; plus he wasn't getting high, nor was he drunk during these odd periods of 'tremor transformation.' As part-owner of his ghost hunting firm in Los Angeles, Resi had established an unblemished personal and working record over several years, until the recent strange changes. He was a proven perfectionist, no doubt about it. That was why he wanted to touch bases with his Girl Friday, Sylph, back home. Something was unfortunately preventing him from doing it. Ordinarily with his Cyplex he could call from anywhere in the world – even a remote jungle wasteland – and reach her without any problem. He'd also sent her several emails from his Silver Bullet laptop, but the results were the same: Non-contact.

The fact was that Resi had suffered recently within the solitary confinement his life had become. Back home some of his friends were curious about the turn his behavior had taken but most dismissed it as a momentary aberration. Everyone had bad stretches from time to time, especially those who dwelled too often in a world of unkind spirits.

All of this strangeness, Resi associated with an earlier time in his life, treating it like a flashback to a period he believed irrevocably trapped in his past. Unreachable, he thought. But now it was upon him with a particular force and contained overtones pertaining to hell-raising student days in Europe when he had drunk, whored, smoked café pot and done a great deal else he cared not to remember. When he returned to America and decided to get serious about his life and future as a working paranormal eye, Resi was able to put the worst behind him and achieve a kind of perspective. All the bad stuff he had done back then was a joke really, something he couldn't be prosecuted for except in a moral realm that hardly mattered in his increasingly immoral homeland.

Resi now had a video cam inside his head which, via his computer, began to depict the most indescribable sensations. He replayed seeing the poet woman's face, then her tormented afflictions from what he assumed was a category of rape. She was imprisoned in that room of pale glowing walls and Resi had been astrally projected inside that room, hovering above Laira's flailing form, unable to stop it. It was a visual stream of consciousness (interrupted from time to time) propelling him to distraction and beyond.

More than anything he was afraid if the optical moments

stopped streaming, something irrevocable might happen to them both and contact with Laira would be lost permanently.

As he walked along towards the Dam, passing a canal or two, Resi kept seeing snatches of things in her room that remained unclear. Obviously there was a man's body there too, with evil intent towards Laira and doing something to her body that seemed more medical than violently sexual. He knew without intuiting more who the man was, causing him further dismay.

Resi had returned to Amsterdam knowing that the badness awaited him again. That cold-heavy night, walking with suitcase in hand from Central Station, he had gravitated almost automatically to the street off Herengracht where the Hotel Nieuw had been ten years before. The round sign bearing the hotel's name jutted out from the building's side just as he remembered. With a clumsy difficulty he had ascended the steep and antiquated stairs to the lobby and bar area. There was still no reception desk and the bartender did all the clerking along with the other hotel duties. Somehow the returning American visitor expected to see Sam Jeffrins there waiting for him, along with Laira McKinney, as if only ten minutes had passed.

In the terribly small bar-room only two young male patrons were at the bar drinking. The bartender was also young – much younger than Resi. They were speaking English and for a moment he believed them American too, not the Canadian and British they were . The bartender, of course, was Dutch and with hardly an upraised eyebrow he greeted the panting Resi.

"A room, please. A single, if you've got one," Resi said, ordering a Heineken.

Per the Magister's wishes, Resi was acting like just another American tourist and hardly there for any investigative business. He tried to warm up at the bar by viewing text messages on his phone and listened to the two patrons discuss the recent soccer games. The homely bar-room was just as before, though perhaps smaller than he recalled it.

"Do you know if Sam Jeffrins is around?" Resi asked the bartender.

"What?"

"Sam Jeffrins. He used to work here, an American."

The apathetic young bartender looked a trifle annoyed while denying any knowledge of Jeffrins. The owner would be in tomorrow and probably could better answer Resi's questions. The hotel was over forty years old, but the owner was a recent one.

Resi said nothing after taking a long swallow of his beer. It was all before this Dutch dude's time, he thought. What if Jeffrins were dead himself? There wouldn't be much to go on. He'd have to deal with the lady who had summoned him all by himself, per usual. Resi was tired and disoriented by the travel and sleeplessness overhanging his life of late. He wanted to punch the bartender out though.

"One hundred Euros," said the bartender routinely.

Resi paid, took the key and picked up his suitcase and tote. The patrons at the bar had stopped talking and eyed him almost curiously. There were ghosts in here they didn't know about that lingered with the cosmic dust of centuries.

He mounted the torturous stairs, the sweat suddenly seeping out all over his body. On the second floor landing there was a painting from the great, Alien War, that had raged in Europe before his time, something Resi knew only from movies, books, and documentaries. The painting depicted a monkey-like creature having many chilling human attributes along with extraterrestrial ones. The Tomu beings, Resi remembered from grade school, were something out of the action comic books during his parents' era. When the war wiped them all out not a trace remained, except scant skeletons that anthropologists still searched for, hoping to unearth another skull to sell to museums. A great controversy had raged after the war as to whether the Tomu actually were extraterrestrial, or just a strange hybrid species of man that had mutated on a distant earth-like planet once colonized by America.

A slight nausea possessed Resi with each step, for he realized his fears were not in the past anymore but up ahead. Struggling with each step for breath, he wondered if this damn hotel wasn't in control of him. He wasn't drunk enough for this, not like in the old days.

A muffled dissonance became more distinct the closer he came to his room on the top landing. The sound was strident – resembling a child's crying – and at first he wanted to believe it was just the mewling of an unsatisfied guest or one more jilted lover perhaps. But Resi knew it wasn't that at all and this knowledge gave him a moment's sour foretaste of things to come.

There up ahead was the room whose number matched the one on his key. Without much hesitation he fought whatever urged him telepathically to gravitate towards the room the crying came from. Resi's body had become ice cold. Was it a boy or woman making the sound?

*Get out of the hotel,* another voice inside him warned. Drop the bags and get the hell out. Something was askew, the crying now became an evil clarion excoriating Resi's nerve center, igniting his brain into a pyrotechnic dance of pixels and shifting shadow. His reason lessened with each step, as did his will.

Resi stood before the door, still fighting the implacable desire to seal his wretched fate He fought monstrously, as did the crying, which evolved into ear assaulting and anarchic waves of insanity. He sensed the door was unlocked, but pressing down on its handle became an effort of labored agony. He was attempting to push down a glistening serpent cast in stone upon a building façade where there was no entrance. Finally the serpent dissolved into liquid matter in his hand and the door opened, revealing the abyss his mind now was, with all its once familiar objects before him.

The crying stopped. Resi's tongue became a reliquary of dust inside his silent mouth. He was staring dumbly at a common hotel room in Holland, at the moment unoccupied by anyone. Nothing corporeal, nothing in the way of earthly spirits was there. It was not his room but some tremor inside wanted him to enter and make it so – and shut the door.

Again he fought an overpowering impulse and stood there stricken. Here before him was the most common hotel furniture: The large bed, the wooden closet, the writing table flanked by two non-descript chairs. The cheap chandelier emitted a fuzz of electric light from the ceiling's center, but was so small it cast hardly any radiance into the room's calcified gloom. Within its spun-glass ornamental goblet a yellowness was captured like some fading artifact. A fetal remnant, Resi reasoned, forever stillborn and listless. A metaphorical offspring of Anne Frank's shadow, of all those incarcerated behind a reality of broken glass, sealed window cages and metal bars, all the structural remains of some ruin no longer habitable except by – what? Nothing really human was in the room, yet something beguiled Resi in a coy manner belonging to an unnatural evil desire.

He closed the door. The serpent was a plain handle again. But the faint stench of disintegrating matter remained in his nostrils as Resi headed towards his own room. Once inside it he hurriedly bolted its door and immediately collapsed next to his bags on the bed. He remained there listening to his own breathing, ruing having come to this watery city, and striving to banish the call that brought him here.

# Chapter 2

# Shades in the Water of Oblivion

Out in the streets that third night, Carlton Resi was again walking into the dark towards a destination he really wasn't sure of, trying in some way to escape the inevitable while surrendering himself to a coldness he associated with the unknown. Such close proximity to the elements and their nexus – with no more old illusions to hide behind – would awaken him to the best course of action to pursue, putting him back on a firm footing to complete his mission.

The cyber-screen which had been a mental window, delicious with color and digital meaning was now off and left Resi facing its dark vision without any real clues. He had been adrift in its oceanic currents and carried to a delusional shore.

The only real thing he'd accomplished of late was making phone contact with the Magister a few hours earlier.

"You're in the Nieuw now I take it?" the Magister's asthmatic voice greeted him. Instead of his actual face appearing in his phone's display there was a Rembrandt self-portrait. One where the old master had his face screwed up in horrific alarm.

"I made it all right. Now all I have to do is locate Jeffrins and find out if Laira's alive or dead.

"What do you think?" the voice rasped back with difficulty.

Resi was standing nearby a shop window the Magister had directed him to in the briefing documents saved on his computer. The shop was a little distance from Canal Street and what he saw displayed behind glass made him suspect more sexual content was being advertised.

"I'm afraid my start here could have gone better, Magister. Earlier I investigated the hotel's interior with some of my electronic devices and was, quite simply, repelled. I recorded some definite spiritual activity near room number 7 but my batteries went dead in a hurry. I got fairly sick, to tell the truth. I'm of the sorrowful impression that Laira McKinney is indeed dead but trying to manifest herself as spiritual energy in a most frightful but perhaps enlightening way."

"You mean she's trying to tell us something."

"In a proverbial manner of speaking she's trying to scream something at us and I think it implicates your Mr. Jeffrins in a, well, perhaps criminal way. Do you happen to know anything about a small boy with red hair at the hotel who may be linked to Laira, by the way?"

There was a lengthy pause of disconcerting heavy breathing before the Magister deigned to reply. "I don't offhand but I'll have one of my aides look into it for you, Resi. Do be careful doing whatever you're doing or about to do. Circumspection is an asset I admire and require for anyone in my employ for whatever duration."

"Right...Now tell me a bit more about your so-called business partner for these new tablets you and he are manufacturing for retail sales. I'm at one of the shop locations by Canal Street."

"And I take it the shop is totally closed with no one in sight prowling about?"

"You got it. All I see in the shop window are a few of the tablets and a sign advertising them as 'SPLANX: THE NEW DIGITAL TABLETS WHERE THE FUTURE BECOMES NOW.'"

"Catchy, isn't it? That slogan, along with all the other pertinent advertising was devised by my colleague and partner, Dr. Hiram de Hazeraux of Belgium. The tablet you're looking at is basically his ingenious invention, probably after stealing most of it from elsewhere. And is something Mr. Samuel Jeffrins is now trying to steal from me."

"You mean he wants the tablets to sell himself?"

"He wants the software and all the bloody codes that make the tablet unique and remarkable. Most of all he wants its control module which, as far as I know, Hiram and only Hiram, remains in possession of. If he ever gets that, we're all in a very bad state, with the business certainly ruined, and God knows what else. He's a blackmailer of extraordinary cunning and I believe he's using Laira as bait to get what he wants. I couldn't tell the police yet, of course, because there is nothing that really points to him as her kidnapper, if indeed that's what he's done. Which I'm almost sure of..."

"So what have the police done so far?"

"Laira McKinney is a missing person officially, is how they're handling it." The Magister paused to cough loudly, a percussion blast in Resi's right ear. "My late stepsister's daughter, who was like my *own*, is officially missing, do you understand?"

"I understand."

"That low-life black market bastard Jeffrins may have murdered her, do you understand?"

"I understand, sir..." Resi had a coughing fit of his own from the cigarette he was hurriedly smoking in the cold. "But, Herr Magister, wouldn't she be more useful to him if she were still alive?"

"I don't think you realize what men like Jeffrins become. You knew him once, that's why I've hired you. Do you think he's changed for the better, Resi? He's beyond dealing with and totally without conscience. His thinking is to eliminate us all because that, to his kind, is the only logic. I've told dear Hiram to lay low for awhile until we see how things go. Of course the release of the tablet to the public is on the backburner now until you find out for me Laira's whereabouts, either in this world or the next."

Resi indicated that he would apprise the Magister of developing details in the coming hours, and continue emailing him updates. As he spoke the display tablet behind the grime-coated window began to more than intrigue him. It too was like one hypnotic vision of what the current digital world was becoming.

Like 3-D but more so, the advertisement declared the user would have a touchscreen producing a variety of sensually stimulating experiences (also invigorating the sexual ones, of course). SPLANX was an actual hands-on way to be transported from the ordinary to the sublime, from any sickness to health, from ignorance to ultimate knowledge. It was more than another tablet, declared the advertisement copy. It was *salvation*, pure and simple.

Earlier that morning Resi had spoken with the current owner of the Hotel Nieuw, a heavyset type who didn't like questions and denied his request to let him do paranormal investigations in the hotel, especially in the room where Laira McKinney's spirit was active. It was closed for renovations, the proprietary, Han van Groot said. Resi had persisted in indirectly getting some information from Van Groot about the whereabouts of ex-friend and fellow American, Sam Jeffrins. Van Groot was a complete blank about everything but remembered the name – yes. Perhaps Jeffrins was connected with the last owners, if remotely. He directed Resi to try his luck at a certain address along the Oude Zids Voorburgwal, or Amsterdam's Red Light district, known as Canal Street. Resi thanked the gruff man with a tip, and later ordered beer for everyone at the bar, while memorizing the address he'd been given.

When he visited that area later in the day, he didn't find what he was looking for. There was no sign of Sam Jeffrins. Instead there were only shuttered buildings apparently, 'at sleep' for the day in a zone which bustled with people after dark. Only a few passers-by were noticeable in daylight, seemingly out of place amblers passing through on their way to a more populated destination. Carlton Resi was just another of them.

Discouraged, the American visitor sought refuge in a nearby café where he drank coffee and debated what to do, all the while getting a second-hand whiff of pot smoke. Perhaps check around, he told himself, and ask more shop people about Jeffrins. Even that would probably garner little more than he already knew. It was nearing mid-afternoon and his searching through the district was proving a failure. But he still had other important addresses to check.

Browsing through a pornography shop, Resi bought a mud-raking tabloid, automatically asking the clerk, "Can you tell me if you know a Sam Jeffrins?"

"What about him?" the preoccupied clerk replied, changing Euros with a no-nonsense swiftness.

"I'm an old friend of his. I'm not a cop, don't worry. I was told he lives at number 107, on this street."

The clerk looked up. "He's gone most of the time."

He continued to stare intently at Resi, as if studying a face where lotto numbers abounded. "Try the address at night. If you find someone there, it will probably be Myri. She can tell you more."

He already had Myri's address, courtesy of the Magister, and planned to visit it that night anyway.

Thereafter, quartering himself in the hotel room, Resi consulted his computer and made notes. Sylph had finally answered his emails and said there were problems of late at the L.A. office; had he been there, they could have likely been avoided. She didn't go into detail about the problems but said she'd tried to call him on the Cypress phone a few times to no avail. Resi shook his head, rubbing his tired face with a sweeping palm, again feeling a strange emanation from the purple screen. He quickly shut it off. There was nothing to do but think and worry about it all while drinking vending machine cans of Heineken. Virtually a prisoner of old world rooms again, he mused, cold despite the jacket he was wearing, and disgruntled because the erratic radiator heat came and went. Then the screaming began anew, rousing Resi from room-shuttered day-mares, revealing him to the room's infinite spaces he would yet try to explore.

Somewhat thereafter, finally his mind was back in the reality of the streets again. The sound of his boot heels thudding upon icy cobblestones became louder in his ears than the incessant city's bustle around him. The night's cruelty was linked to that great concatenation of the unknown threatening to submerge him in its inhuman tidal force. Why fight what doesn't seem right, he asked, even if it's a natural commandment? Like everything else, the question was now inconceivable to understand. Time had become a mega-blur, making it impossible for Resi to tell what hour he was consistently really in.

Returning to O.Z. Voorburgwal, the nocturnal sight greeting him was indeed a different one from daytime. The narrow passageways teemed with people parading between rows of buildings and canals. Resi recalled how it had been several years before when he'd walked these streets as an exchange student, hunting prostitutes. They'd always doubtlessly be there and it perplexed Resi to see some of the younger ones, who were children the last time he'd caroused through here, hitting bar after bar, his body sodden with the beer his despair was never dissipated by. Now Resi was cold sober and the girls were grown, used, even hard-looking. A fallen lot of daughters, but if he ever had one she'd end up here and Resi knew he'd never be able to find her.

He was looking for anyone who could tell him about the Hotel Nieuw and the woman's shade inhabiting it which had called him there. He could still hear her ill laughter (a mocking thing, a sad thing) and knew it would increase if, by chance, she were watching his inept trek now from an upper story window no horny sailor, who wasn't a ghost could reach. Again Resi was compelled to confront something he'd managed to avoid – but could no longer.

The presence of perambulating males alive with obscene cheer sickened him. When he was propositioned to buy hashish by a young African, shabbily dressed, who spoke with low-voiced mellifluous urgency, Resi could only stare back at a figure that should rightfully belong to his past but had escaped. In turn the African quickly sidled away from this intruder who resembled a madman on the prowl for something not found in this eternal brackish stagnancy of dive bars and whorehouses.

To supplicate the divine is to suffer like an animal – or something to that effect, Resi mused, paraphrasing something he'd once read, something which had never made sense to him. To partake of my swinging dick is what Sam Jeffrins would say. Standing before that man's purported address again, Resi looked upon the same drab building façade that now – at street level – had three open and lit picture windows for customers to view the ladies sitting within. Of course this was where Jeffrins would be, Resi laughed, in a house of prostitutes. The whore staring back at him from behind her window was in her late twenties, wearing a skimpy, sequined black bra and matching panties, with a gossamer-thin blouse wrapped loosely around her shoulders. She idly stared back at Resi as if they were species of fish life observing each other from different ends of an aquatic prism. Her made-up (but not very beautiful) face remained impassive through this lengthy staring, broken only by Resi's panting vapor hovering like a misty exclamation point in the cold. The only movement was an elaborate crossing of her legs in their reddish nylon stockings.

*Well?* Her eyes spoke.

He motioned for her to open the door, which she did reluctantly, due to the cold.

"Could you give me some…information?" Resi asked. "I can pay you," he said over his smoker's cough, extracting from his jacket a money clip of Euros, on hand for such occasions. The somewhat weary woman allowed his entry, quickly closing the door after him to bolt out the air.

"You're Myri, aren't you?"

There was no surprise at being recognized in her eyes. Myri slowly lit a cigarette then drew the curtains across the large picture window. Resi could still see the outlined parade of men shuffling by. Now it was warmer in the small room and somewhat cozier. Myri turned to regard her visitor, the cigarette in her hand raised upward in a sophisticated manner. She made Resi feel like a voyeur who had stumbled into her world.

"I only want to ask some questions about Sam Jeffrins."

Resi placed some Euros on the small bureau laden with perfume bottles and other cosmetic articles. She silently continued to scrutinize him through a drifting layer of smoke.

"Are you police or what?"

"Oh no, nothing such as that, though I'm an investigator of paranormal activity back in California..."

Resi made coughing noises again. He stood there uncomfortably, removing his gloves and feeling older than this woman, though they were close in age.

"What do you want with Sam?"

"What do I want with Sam. He's an old friend from student days I haven't seen in a long time and" – Resi shrugged nonchalantly – "I'd like to see him again."

"Oh, I see. It's a sentimental occasion. Not what I've heard."

This Dutch whore with her fine English and studied manner began to irritate Resi. He took a closer look at her, slyly studying the hairline above her pallid brow, noting the auburn tresses cascading over her shoulders. Her features were too pale and unblemished for her trade, yet heavy with make-up. She was on the verge of nodding into a perpetual languor one must never succumb to. Resi didn't like her. She was a sly mockery of established female virtues. Her mouth was a crimson slash whose sharp teeth had bitten the tongues of lost loves. Not to forget her half-ass negligee, a throw-away coverlet decorated by doves flying from a cleavage of false breasts.

"I've never met a paranormal investigator before."

"Oh really…?"

Resi felt like he needed a drink. He glanced at the quilt-covered divan nearby. He could see himself in the dust-fringed mirror. A disoriented and haggard trespasser into something he should get out of. He'd been here before, in the proverbial other lifetime and marveled sardonically that he was really catching up with all the hustlers in the world.

"Please tell me about Sam Jeffrins, when he'll be back."

She smiled. "I'll tell you something. My husband isn't Sam Jeffrins."

"I didn't think so."

She extinguished the cigarette with slow vengeance before brushing away ash with yellow fingers stained by nicotine, then crossed her arms authoritatively to regard Resi.

"There are a lot of people who work for Sam around here. Did you know that?"

"No – I didn't."

"Even my husband does sometimes," she joked in that conning manner Resi found distasteful. But at last he was getting somewhere, and she appeared to believe him. "He's very well known around here, and does enough business."

For an instant Resi didn't know if she were discussing her husband or Jeffrins, but opted for the latter.

"Yes, Sam has been in Amsterdam a long time," said Myri."Many people come to see him. Not everybody will get to see him, however. Not even the Magister."

They went on talking for a while with Resi collecting as many factual bits as he could. A sudden glimmer cast her features into a more serious light. She was part of the overall action.

"Go to this bar on the end corner across from Central Station. Ask for him there. Maybe they'll tell you. You can mention me, and say you like the trending cosmos. Sometimes he's there…"

Resi put on his gloves.

"Thanks."

"If you knew more about women, you'd know more about Sam Jeffrins," she said, opening the door for him. "Funny, isn't it?"

Resi didn't answer. He didn't want to slip back. The past was unreachable, the deceitful truth long buried and the quest for Jeffrins a vicious circle, leading him nowhere except into the orbit holding him. Yet he kept moving, consulting his phone for text messages, hoping against hope. The circus of humanity around him was the panoply of stark colors Van Gogh might have mixed on his palette. The ancient building walls blurred into old sepia shadows interspersed with chromatic bits of iridescent blue, evident in the canals shining with an underwater eeriness all the way. Resi was caught in a diffracted spectrum intimating ineffable secrets that lived only with the night on Canal Street. Lost and never found again, he told himself, going into the bar Myri had told him about.

# Chapter 3

# Make it One More for My Baby

It was just another waterfront dive bar, populated by the same seedy male characters who appeared to exist everywhere. At the north end of the bar Resi found a vacant stool and ordered a beer after finally getting the busy barmaid's attention. Sitting there he felt out of his element and depressed by the bar's atmosphere; crowded and grossly smelling. At present a rousing native song blasted an anthem for all maritime veterans. There were areas in the Netherlands decimated by the Alien War, needing refurbishment after suffering long neglect. It was even in the news blaring from the mammoth TV no one watched above the bar mirrors. Resi could have gone on listing what he disliked about everything and everyone there. Instead he drank, warming up and trying to marshal his energies for what had to be done.

He sat nursing his beer and watched the barmaid who smoked a thin cigar. She appeared to be listening to a scruffy pair of elderly Dutchmen reciting their woes in a monotone of disenchantment. Leaving the drunkenly argumentative pair, the barmaid sidled closer to Resi's end of the bar.

"Want another?"

Resi realized his glass was drained of beer. He nodded and she efficiently poured him another glass full while sweeping up his Euros with one fluid movement. Awakened somewhat by this professional dexterity, Resi looked at her face again. It was moon-shaped, almost coarse, and there was a punk-like piece of jagged silver attached to the right ear lobe. Her rusty colored hair was very long and so straight it might well be ironed. With her once broken nose, prominent cheek bones and Mongoloid profile, was she possibly a descendant of that hybrid generation that germinated after the Alien conflict? If so, she had better have her papers in order, Resi knew, or she'd be banished from the city otherwise.

"You look like you could use a good year's sleep," she told him.

"I've had a few long days." Resi sighed.

She told him she was only filling in for an hour or two. Tending bar was hardly her trade, she said with another of her familiar looks. She was really lead singer in a Rock band from Hamburg. "Have you been out partying on Canal Street?"

"I'm looking for somebody..."

Resi said it in a tired and uncaring manner, like someone searching for an item in a desk drawer. When he mentioned he was a paranormal investigator the barmaid said, "No Way," snapping her head back coltishly. Her perfume was pure sweat and her long, curved fingernails were coated with miniature floral designs painted in silver.

Resi laughed, tapping his forehead like a psychic. He explained a little why he wanted to see Sam Jeffrins, giving his own name and some background filler. He ordered yet another drink, knowing he could get drunk at this rate.

"Is my man dead or alive?"

"He's around sometimes," Ms. Mongoloid answered, though not too convincingly. "He's part-owner of the bar, you know."

Oh really, Resi wanted to say, but didn't. The barmaid left abruptly to service other customers, leaving behind a looming smoke cloud for Resi to contemplate. And through it, in the growing stupor from his alcoholic intake, Resi strained at the sight of a seated figure some yards away, within a small alcove in the kitchen directly behind the bar. The heavyset figure was seated alone at a broken table and apparently staring too, and Resi kept straining to focus its features into a recognizably remembered face.

Tranquilly sitting there and partaking of a quiet meal, there was a poignant contentedness in the solitary diner's manner. A good sight indeed for any believers in the famous Dutch *gezel-ligheid*...Resi watched almost enviously as the seated diner rose brusquely from his table, disrupting the picturesque tableau so vibrant with its tonal hues. He combed his long bushy hair, put on a red stocking cap and walked towards the bar.

"I recognize you, pal."

"Hello, Sam Jeffrins."

"What the hell are you doing here, Resi?"

Resi held up his empty glass. "Drinking — "

Jeffrins had the glass immediately refilled.

"On the house..."

"Thanks. Have one on me."

"I drink free here anyway," Jeffrins said, filling a glass with Heineken. "Just buy our cigars."

"Good enough."

Resi watched the stocky figure of Jeffrins moving about, occasionally trading words with other bar patrons, even taking the barmaid's place behind the bar now and then. He noted that Jeffrins was a little heftier, but not as fat around the middle as he remembered. Also his long russet hair was concealed under a cap for a change, but the cherubic yet tough-looking face remained unshaven. It was still Sam Jeffrins, yet something told Resi it could not completely be him. The years took their toll on everyone in ways that added up to identity theft. The Magister would compliment his eye for detail when Resi emailed his report later.

"Another brew for my Einstein," Jeffrins ordered after returning.

They watched each other drink through an eye-burning curtain of cigarette smoke that was growing heavier with each moment.

"How long you going to be in Amsterdam, Resi?"

"...A few days."

"Just reminiscing, is that it?"

"I suppose just that."

"What do you think of my bar along Zeedijk?"

"The best in town, I guess…In the right place too."

"You better believe it. Nothing will ever change this town."

Jeffrins lit the cigar Resi gave him and squinted back. "You look cold as some bitch without a mother."

"I've been spoiled by all that Southern California sun."

Jeffrins leaned forward. "And all those warm women with long yellow hair at the beach."

"You got it, buddy," replied Resi, flashing thumbs-up like homeboys do on the block.

Jeffrins snorted, smoking intensely, then said above the drone of nearby conversation: "You want' a know something, Resi? When I knew you back then you were a pretty fucked-up dude, with your head up your asshole. I only recognized you because Lovely told me you were here."

"Thanks a lot."

"But I'll say this." Jeffrins poked a long-nailed forefinger at his visitor, a habitual gesture, usually with the same hand holding his cigar. "You look like you know a goddamn lot more then you knew then. You've been sniffin' out those ghosts all right! I like all that spooky shit. What else you been up to?"

"Working…living."

"That impresses the hell out of me."

"I'm stayin' at the old hotel…you know the one I mean. I hear you were in good there, Sam, once upon a time."

Resi could tell the reaction of his ex-friend wasn't a good one. He would try to decipher Jeffrins for what he needed, finish his beer and leave, immediately calling the Magister. Jeffrins was already brushing him off in a manner reserved for the inessential. The brutish barmaid with the nasty hair-do returned and Jeffrins began a lively conversation with her, repeatedly calling her 'Jolie' in a familiar manner as she resumed her tasks and once more the bar-room was alive with raucous laughter and insultingly provocative remarks. The aged and walnut-stained walls were a homely *pilsjes*-like color, and the blur of foam began to swim in Resi's eyes as he struggled for control. Same old Sam Jeffrins after all, only the locale and the fashions changed. Resi felt as alienated as ever sitting there on his raggedy stool, alone, for the most part, in the din.

Then something in him began to somersault. His senses snapped away from a continuity of perception and his mind began to slumber, out of time.

Faces pitched back and forth in his memory with an alarming movement. He was looking into the light show his consciousness had become. The present was the past and any differentiation between those notions was abolished by the mewling revel of one great sensory montage threatening to implode within him at any second, sending his future into unknown oblivion.

He reached up, trying to grapple with unknown apparitions dissolving before his eyes and eluding the strafing futility of his fingertips. He kept reaching out nonetheless, increasingly panicked by the sensation of impotence overtaking him with its mindless and implacable ferocity, and realized slowly he was drowning in a firmament of fear which ebbed from the maze of canals around him.

Helplessly, there in a realm of kinetic abandon assaulting him from some cybernetic void, Carlton Resi felt their hands pinioning his body and brusquely slapping the life in him away and back, despite the onrushing tears of dismay. He was 'God,' the hands were of God, that libation being splashed about him was a holy water he had always thirsted for. Let it submerge his lungs fatally, he didn't care. All that mattered was his struggle to be reborn now through the cyber mortality he experienced, and he was not afraid of death. Death suddenly had a face he had to accept and Resi realized that face belonged to Sam Jeffrins.

In an instant the struggle stopped.

"Chill yourself down, Wop. You got to chill yourself down.

Wreck any of my furniture and I'll let lovely Jolie clean up on you. Okay? Just chill yourself down."

"I will," Resi said, shocked but amazed to be lying there, on some couch in his bath of alcoholic sweat, still dazed in the cyber ethers of that virus he knew had emanated from his computer, and feeling the iron clamp of brutal hands imprisoning his wrists. The strength there of a man who beat women and might well have killed Laira McKinney was evident in the cyber flashes of the drugged dream his life had become.

"You drank too much, Wop. It's my fault. I should've stopped Jolie from feeding you those different shots. But what the hell, it's your necktie party…"

Resi forced a grimace. "I need to know…you and Laira…what you did…"

"Jolie's bringing out some coffee, man…Just chill down."

"I have, Jeffrins, believe me…I have."

Resi looked around, having come back, and recognized the homely interior of an apartment. He felt his heart pulsing back to normal and sighed. You're some fucking investigator, he told himself. He had really blown it, no doubt about that. And being unable to document the activity of unknown spirits in an old Amsterdam hotel scheduled soon for demolition was another stroke of his genius to ruin his reputation. Nobody but his psychiatrist back in Beverly Hills would buy it.

With his peripheral vision he saw Jolie emerging from the kitchen with a coffee tray and realized she was almost bigger than Jeffrins. She was another freak and Resi despised the fact.

Jeffrins was sitting at a table across from Resi and fiddling with the Cyplex phone. "I'll need this now, Wopper. Don't freak out about it." He continued smoking in his intense fashion as Jolie served the prostrate captive on the couch. "You never could hold your liquor, son, and you even screw up your electronics. What the fuck? Hope you don't mind we brought you here, but we figured it was better then heave you in the canal."

"Thanks a lot," Resi said, though it sounded like a sarcastic comment. "And don't fuck with my phone, I'll need it back." To his amazement he learned it was nearing dawn in another white room by the train station.

"Hope you enjoyed your unconscious rest, fucker."

Resi, now observed his captor, whose features were mutating into grotesque, shimmering patterns of pure ugliness. *Strange brew, look what's inside of you,* he recalled the song going. There was a roseate *schemerlampen* on the nearby table, and its emanation gradually overtook all color in the room, so that his eyes had the sensation of being inside a multi-faceted, prismatic ruby.

He struggled not to let the frenzy of it all overcome him, though it had become an energy with a mind, direction, and purpose all its own. *Whatever it was...*And was the tech freak Jeffrins and his geeks responsible for it? Resi was becoming an instrument of his own pain that others turned on and off.

He turned, then saw the face and form of the young barmaid, Jolie, also being affected and transmuted garishly by this unique radiance, now rendered an androgynous ectoplasm with fibril-lating nerve ends. *I'm losing it again,* Resi told himself, realizing the emanation was a single-toned, ever increasing sound wave inside and beyond him. Something embodying that unmitigated screaming he associated with the ethereal and deceased Laira in her endless agony, which – never fully articulated – was something unworldly to its very core, and how unknowable?

Jolie pulled off her wig with a muscular movement. Her mouth opened to expose great white cliffs of Dover teeth for him. A noxious yellow fluid the color of a despoiled amaranth slithered from her mouth. She unbuttoned her sweater to reveal the swaying crimson tendrils of something Resi could only associate with an unclassified beast.

"I'm in full-bodied heat, man," she told him, flapping an icy blue eyelid into one exaggerated wink.

"She's one of God's beautiful creations," Resi could hear Sam Jeffrins say, almost sentimentally. "This calls for a drink, Jolie."

Without hesitation he began sucking the bloody tendrils on her chest, his tongue riveted to them.

"Drinks all around," Jolie responded through heaving sighs. Her eyelids melted away in the electric heat of passion, revealing black holes of nothingness.

"Doubles all around," Jeffrins concurred, pouring strong liquor into water glasses. His mutating form still wavered before Resi's vision. "And some Geneva gin to go with the occasion, because we're almost there," he announced quietly, bringing the glasses forward.

One was placed in Resi's trembling, roseate hand. He wondered what it could be doing there, the hand holding the glass which was his and yet another's. He wondered what the liquid might be that caused such disintegration in the forms before him. The liquid would drown him, Resi decided, and he could not possibly drink it. He'd already consumed something inside this doll's house of an apartment, and his mind and body swam because of it. Resi could not possibly drink anything more. Another draft would be fatal, he warned himself. Laira had just told him so. Wafting in the drink itself, she told him how Jeffrins had implanted her in the Nieuw's white hotel room before everything became the color of darkness. Yet he had succumbed unconsciously before, and now he was consciously doing so, despite everything, until the difference between those once separated states was delusional at best. He dwelled, at that moment, in a holistic hell of poisoned senses and his fear formed an impregnable barrier against any reason.

Toasting him, both Jeffrins and Jolie drank deeply. They might as well be fucking ghouls, Resi knew.

"You killed Laira McKinney at the Nieuw, Sam. You implanted her with the same stuff oozing from chesty over there, didn't you?"

"You're full of shit. I don't go to that hotel anymore."

"But you were there that night, that very special night. Weren't you? Without question, buddy, you were. Doing it so her abduction and assimilation to whatever took her in the fields would occur...Because she would leave that place screaming like she'd been raped."

"That's bullshit, Wop, and you know it. What the hell's wrong with you? What are you on, man?"

Resi stared back, trying to place the face, whatever beamed maliciously down upon him, an Aztec god's mask behind a rushing flame. He pushed himself up on his elbows, struggling with it.

"There's something in the past...waiting to be born again. Something you're a part of and helping, you son of a bitch."

"What the hell are you talking about, you fucking Wop?"

"She was young...she worked in the old hotel for a while. A blonde, beautiful young Dutch-born girl, don't you remember? She had secrets to keep. And she wanted to be an artist, a poet, like some chosen do. Don't you remember? You told me you wanted to marry her, instead of that barmaid bitch you obviously never did...Because she had hair on her chest?"

"Too bad you're no Irishman," replied Sam Jeffrins. "I think you're definitely out of line, boy. I'd believe you more if you were still drunk – but you ain't. Too fuckin' bad...You'd probably get more respect." Jeffrins took down a heavy swallow of his gin and continued staring back levelly with a feral impersonality, and outright ice cold calculation in his expression. "But you're sick. Know that? You're flyin' on some bad shit from stuff you can't handle anyway, just like the good old student days, though it's a miracle you can even talk back, know that?"

"I know what you don't want me to know, and what I've been paid to find out."

"So what are you gonna do about it?" asked Jeffrins, watching his Jolie's shadowy form twitch about, her sinuous shape becoming blurred by the omnipresent radiating paleness. He was on his feet, poised like a boxer expecting a blow, hands ready at his sides.

"I'm not going to do a goddamn thing," Resi answered, getting to his feet slowly and unsteadily in the now colorless room. Its painterly light was draped at the wall corners by the chiaroscuro of some unreal darkness. Her voice inside emboldened him, aided him in keeping some equilibrium navigating through the waves from the vortex of supernatural forces Laira called from. "I just want you to tell me, as somebody who once knew her too, why she's dead…And how she got that way."

"You're a crazy, goddamn Wop, Resi. That's the sad fucking fact! Nothing can change that. I don't know why I don't ram this bottle through your puked-on face." Jeffrins let a short but deriding burst of laughter underline his outburst. "I mean you are one *sorry* fuck. Okay? The fact is, you can't get your own ass screwed, so you want somebody to do it for you. Do you think you've found the light? I'm surprised you ain't in here with a bible and a beanie on." His hoarse laughter ensued, devolving slowly into chagrined wheezing. "How the hell do I know what happened to your princess or whoever the fuck you're talkin' about, hey —?" Jeffrins lapsed into silence, shaking his head before putting his hands on his ample hips.

Resi was still disbelieving and kept lurching forward. "Didn't you do a passionate number on the lady in question in the name of your criminal science?"

Jeffrins picked up his glass and deposited its contents in Resi's face. "You're full of it, pal." In the disgruntled interval's air they regarded one another in silence. The dripping gin glistened on Resi's cheek, adding moisture to his sweat-stained features. Jeffrins laughed now, staring at him. "Why don't you lick that up? You might get a buzz."

"You helped transform her into another dimension, Jeffrins, the same as dealing her a death blow. Because they wanted her, needed her desperately for whatever reason...There must be high stakes involved for you to have done it."

Jeffrins wanted to laugh again, but a virulent anger got the better of him. "You should a never come back to Amsterdam, Resi. Times have changed and you can't change them back. Some things you can't bring back. Well you and her fit that category. You should a never come back, and now you gotta follow it through. The vacation's over, and you've had your day." The brief, watchful silence became heavily charged. "So get the sweet hell out. I'm letting you go."

Resi nodded at the wavering form in the corner shadows. "Is that what your manly flower wants? Or is it still trying to figure out what sex it is?"

"You fuckin' bitch," Jeffrins said, shaking his head, then stepped forward to level his fist against Resi's chest.

"Don't kill him, honey," said Jolie, her insincere voice thrown out like a ventriloquist's.

"He'll grow tits before that'll happen," Jeffrins said, ready to deliver another haymaker Resi's way.

Resi was reaching for something he felt might be the handle to another door: A white, dully-beaming instrument mired in the protoplasm of shadow cells. Somehow his hand covered a million intricately veined crosshatchings forming a grand and unknowable design.

But there was *nothing* now – only night – and he was back in it alone, bleeding and staggering, heading for a hotel he couldn't reach again. If he could, maybe he'd find the handle of something only Laira could give, if she weren't in fact an image of the same beast he feared was trying to kill him.

# Chapter 4

# To Perceive the Totality of Being in a Cup of Tea

He knew where Myri stayed during the day when she wasn't a dry hustler on Canal Street. The address she'd written down for him was on the crumpled scrap of paper in his pocket. She'd given it too him that ill-fated night because he was, she could see, a man who was not going to stay out of trouble. Staying out of trouble didn't apply to him, Resi believed, since he was mostly always in it. A karmic fate was at issue here, and it was guided by a power which defied conventional rationality. He had tried to explain it to her, but the young prostitute wasn't receptive to such intimations. She said he looked ill enough as was, and warned him there were bad things on the street. Resi had replied that night that he'd never been cleaner in his life. The days when he was into bad things were a thing of the past.

After searching the Canal Street environs for sometime, Resi finally found her sitting in an Indonesian café she had indicated was her haunt around noonday. It was only 11 am, but she was sitting alone at a small table with a picture window view of the street. Almost like she was waiting for someone, Resi decided. Now more sedate-looking than the hardcore version of the whore he'd first encountered, when he had learned she was only in the business part-time. (The rest of the time she was busy with duties as a freelance decorator of nearby apartments, a complete contrast with her street life.) By her cool demeanor, greeting his arrival with little overt expression, Resi figured he'd failed to impress her, or she probably met loads of men like this, here in the pleasant and opulent restaurant interior.

"So there you are," she said calmly, critically observing his facial bruises. She had a displeased expression which bore merci-

34

lessly in on Resi now. "I see you've met Jeffrins. You don't look so good."

"I need to sleep some, but I did have my first encounter with him."

"So was it productive or what?"

Resi sat down, though he wasn't invited to, appearing furtively uncomfortable all the while. "If processing info is productive, I processed much." As Myri gave a light, basically uncomplimentary laugh, Resi looked around for an available waiter.

"Can you stand a breakfast of some kind?"

"My stomach collided with some fists unfortunately. Some of that hot coffee should do me. Fact is, I don't even know if my stomach can handle that. I think I'm hungry, but a little too queasy to eat."

Myri lit a cigarette and eyed him. "You are a poor boy indeed. I'm sure your queasiness prevents you from doing a great many things sometimes."

"I've only been queasy lately. Since this business started."

Resi produced more Euro notes before her, telling Myri he needed to know more about everything, and then asked her about Laira McKinney.

"I saw her a few times with Jeffrins. You know how poorly he acts around women. It was mostly at the Nieuw or his dive bar."

A bespectacled young waiter arrived, and Resi ordered his coffee, coughing somewhat abjectly.

"I'm glad I found you again. I don't have many friends at the moment."

"Just those you pay to be. Did you have a long search?"

"Not that long. Your directions are good. I like walking."

"People get lost in this city even if they know about it."

"I suppose so," Resi answered. "I'm not going to go into detail about what I found out about Jeffrins."

"Everybody knows he's into the black market and has shady

dealings with foreign enterprises never to be mentioned in his presence."

"So I found out. But I need to know more about his acquaintances, names, or phone numbers, anything you can get me. It's starting to become an urgent matter."

The waiter returned, presenting Resi with a cappuccino he tested before taking a real swallow. It was not to his liking. "When your system needs flushing out, you can't drink anything. The drinks Jeffrins gave me were like homemade hooch from hell. I'd like to know where he keeps his merchandise, like any warehouse or storage units. This guy is up to kinky stuff big time."

Myri kept staring quietly back at him, not able to fully express the distaste she felt. "You should be careful of how much you learn, Resi. In this city people have fared better learning less."

"I don't deny those are words to live by. That could be the subject of our next brunch."

Resi rose from his bamboo chair, saluting her with a flippant gesture. He coughed over his affected laughter. "You know, what I really need right now is a gun. I couldn't get one through airport screening."

"I hope you're not going to shoot up Canal Street."

Resi's laugh became sarcastic. "You're a wise one, lady. Secretly I think you ladies and the Magister run this town, and Sam Jeffrins is only second banana."

"You feel so unprotected you need a gun in a city where they're outlawed?"

"This job might warrant it, even for a paranormal investigator."

"Job…! You cowboys make it a sport, shooting up everything. It's become an international sport."

"We all need protection, even you."

"Oh really, is that it? I for one trust our police. I highly do not recommend you acquire a gun, my friend. Not with the luck you've had so far."

"But you do know where I can discreetly get one? I'll pay extra for it."

"I'm not charging you anything. I'm telling you not to get a gun for obvious reasons."

"Then you won't help me? And you don't believe Jeffrins and that fright wig of a moll of his have it in for me while I stay in town?"

"Then leave this town, won't you."

"You're a kept specimen, a beautiful woman, and some joker like me comes along trying to help free somebody's spirit from this oblivion, somebody a little better than us who got her neck accidentally broken because she wouldn't become another whore on Canal Street?"

She continued gazing at Resi throughout his tirade. An expression somewhere on the edge of her unblinking eyes told him he was transgressing. Her lips tightened and she said: "That's what you really think? And that happened a long time ago, didn't it?"

"Some things don't get swept away, do they, especially in matters of injustice? Funny how everything around here becomes ancient history after only a day or two…"

"You're becoming almost more intriguing, Mr. Resi. Do you think you're some kind of avenger hunting down old Nazis? Let me tell you something. You don't know enough about this vengeance crusade that is more than a job for you. People die every day for whatever reason, here and all over creation. How much have you really personally suffered? We have put up with everything throughout our history, including a foiled invasion by an alien species. Please don't tell me about it. It all comes under the category of tough luck, and thank you very much not."

When the waiter returned, Resi picked up the bill and left.

It was a pleasant enough place in the *grachtenhuizen* nearby the

Plantage Middenlaan. It was pleasant enough, Resi thought, as far as four storied antiquated buildings go, and the atmosphere of bourgeois respectability had its comforting effect.

Resi had devoured – alone – a good lunch of *koffietafel*, having finally regained his appetite, then had frittered away the bulk of this overcast, gray afternoon awaiting his appointment with the Magister. He had taken the tram from Central Station: A scenic mode of transport winding its way through the city's heart, and even though he'd had trouble getting off at the right stop, he was able to double-back a few blocks on foot. To his sore-footed amazement, Rezi eventually discovered the address he wanted a good fifteen minutes before the hour, in plenty of time for the dismal tea-taking ritual he was sure awaited him.

Resi was greeted at the door by an elderly female servant with a disapproving mien. Nonetheless upon stating his name he was admitted into a teakwood foyer smelling of musty artifacts, with the soothing effect one encounters leaving a bustling street scene to enter a domestically preserved world. The servant (in her everyday livery of provincial stripe) took his overcoat and told him to wait until she informed the Magister of his arrival.

It was warm inside the pastel-hued foyer and Resi gratefully waited. He occupied the moments by staring at some framed daguerreotypes of local harbor life which looked a cut above what one would find at the flea market. Were these expensive antiques Resi was looking at? His unknowing eye couldn't tell, but there was a heirloom air about it all, as if the flowered vases, pendent wall clock, and filigreed knick-knacks had been handed down from family to family through the years.

The servant returned and requested the slightly disoriented visitor to follow her. Resi obediently did, and soon found himself inside a rather large study even more filled with priceless items and arty objects.

Sitting at a large desk in his contemplative majesty, the dignified form of the Magister was squinting at a large window.

His hands were clasped almost clerically on his chest, and he was attired in an impressive ensemble of sorts: An immaculate brown coat with matching vest complimented his expensive shoes, jewelry, and accessories. His scant white beard betrayed a wrinkled chin beneath the terrain of his face. Yes, Resi thought, he was something forbidding and out of Rembrandt now and then all right.

The Magister turned slightly to acknowledge this intrusion into his sanctuary and Resi could see how his avuncular visage bore the repose of one who endures life for the most part in solitude and silence. With his neatly coiffed hair almost manicured – so that not one gray uneven strand remained – the Magister's blue eyes were like jewels plucked from a preserving vat of alcohol. *You've seen that man before,* Resi thought, extending his hand to one whose respectability exuded a genial, bloodhound quality...*But in what lifetime?*

"Please bring us the tea now, Judith," the Magister instructed his servant after she had made the announcement. "And Mr. Resi – please come in and sit down."

Resi did as advised, accepting the clasping fingers of the Magister's elegantly extended right hand. It was gloved, he noted in perturbation, within a pliable brown material resembling deerskin. More perturbing was the fact the Magister did not rise upon meeting Resi, as if some unknown protocol forbade it.

"Sit, sit!" the Magister advised with good-natured impatience, indicating a brass-studded chair with a creaking frame. "If Myri is wrong about you being an honorable chap, then I'll shoot you myself."

"Thanks for directing me to her, though I haven't had a turbulent free go of things," Resi replied, somewhat lamely, to cover his growing perplexity at the Dutch peculiarities of the Magister. They were already comparable to Eleusinian mysteries – and perhaps more unknowable.

"Of that I'm quite sure, and sorry to hear, Resi," the Magister admitted. He extracted cigars from an ornate humidor crested by the silver figure of a winged female goddess. Briskly he cut them with small scissors before handing one to his guest.

Resi couldn't refrain from inventorying the Magister's suit, replete with two-toned tie, stickpin, and exquisite emerald cufflinks. The Magister was dressed more for a business meeting than an afternoon of tea with a paranormal investigator from America.

"Smoke!" he said, peremptorily passing a sterling lighter Resi's way. Though no cigar smoker, Resi accepted it obediently. Pleased, the Magister lit his cigar with a savoring regard.

"Not bad, eh?" the Magister inquired, watching Resi stoke his imported stogie to a smoky red crackle. "Bad for my asthma, I know...but what the devil."

"Excellent."

"Indeed!" the Magister concurred, examining his own cigar through a layer of wafting smoke. "The brand however escapes me. I simply tell Judith to make sure the tobacconist supplies us with the most exotic imported specials. And then I'm satisfied."

"Without question," agreed Resi, feeling like a regal cigar smoker, though overwhelmed by smoke.

Shortly thereafter Judith returned bearing a large tray with a suitably ornate tea service. In taciturn dutifulness she set about preparing the service, setting cup, saucer, silverware, and serviette before Resi. Having properly set the guest's service, she repeated the procedure with more elegant affectation for the Magister, who forbearingly watched her. The Magister himself prepared his tea in a ceramic kettle of art nouveau design, punctiliously straining and pouring it with exactitude. It was obviously his daily and personal ritual.

"You have had some trouble with Jeffrins, but at least you've found him," the Magister remarked through the tea drinking. The sound of their stirring spoons was interrupted occasionally by his delicate, connoisseur-like sips and swallows. Resi wished he could have more ably emulated the Magister, but continued only going through the motions. He knew that was the saga of life anyway.

"He wanted me to find him of course."

"Is that so? But you've made progress, and your excellent report tells me a lot. I know now that my unfortunate lady in question, dear Laira, is now of the spirit world as you put it. But I don't think the police will buy it until her actual remains come to light."

"Your Mr. Jeffrins has a clue to their whereabouts for sure, if he hasn't already permanently disposed of them," the Magister allowed, his face becoming a grim mask.

"I'm afraid this is getting quite grim, Resi. Are you certain you're capable of proceeding? I'm sorry I didn't stress our using more discretion when I talked to you on the phone last night. I was upset and angry."

Resi lowered his tea cup, staring morosely into its contents. He thought the Magister had been a little cavalier upon learning his Laira was dead. "I have had contact with her spirit at least twice. She's trying to warn us about something. It's the little boy with the red hair who puzzles me."

"What can I do to help you?"

"I'd like to do some research in your personal library, if you don't mind."

"Of course…It's both digital and contains thousands of press books. I'll have Judith take you there. What exactly will you be researching?"

"All I can about the Alien War that took place in the Netherlands, and everything that mostly followed. And anything I can find out about Laira's heritage and family."

"You think all that has a bearing on what that scum Jeffrins has been up to?"

"Yes, I do," said Resi, though the Magister's face clearly

questioned it. "What's occurred isn't some crime of passion, but part of a criminal procedure in progress. The further it goes, the more you'll have to fear. It possibly will adversely affect your own corporate interests and financial stability in this town."

The Magister exhaled smoke and stared. There was no longer a genial bemusement on his features. "Is that so? But Jeffrins is simply the black market. I have no connections there he can use against me, you must know that."

"Everyone seems intertwined in this town, Magister, like hounds at the same watering hole. There is something behind Jeffrins I need to find out about, a something much bigger than him, perhaps. Or even anyone. Whatever's steering him into doing what he's done or plans to do. And he wants me to continue doing what you've hired me to do, ironic as that may strike you."

"On the phone you said Jeffrins is potentially engaged in international terrorism. He's always been homegrown in the black market only. It wouldn't make sense for him to attack our own economy. How could that make him rich, and once he's definitely a known part of such activity, what then?"

"Myri has given me names of middle east terrorists he's connected with, or certainly renegade types he's done business with. He's taken his enterprise to a whole new level, or is trying to. He wants to unseat you."

The Magister angrily lowered his cigar, shaking his head.

"Also, I will need to arm myself, sir. You'll have to see to that as soon as possible. I'm in a somewhat compromised position here it seems which I can't allow to get worse."

"My dear young fellow," the Magister began somberly, "Myri told me you're a very confused young man at the moment, with some delusion about seeing gremlins and all that. She tells me you even fear her in a way, which will prove insupportable in my opinion if it continues. I need her…"

"To maintain some leverage on Canal Street, Herr Magister? I know it's all perfectly legal there, but..."

"To maintain some leverage on Canal Street?" the Magister said mockingly, as if such a statement was preposterous in the extreme.

Resi almost bit his tongue before pushing his tea cup and saucer away with finality.

"Sir, I'm glad you got Myri's version of things. Do you believe her? I know you think I'm in a hypertensive state. I appreciate your previous understanding and this hospitality, and hope you'll forgive any indiscretion I've made, but at some point Jeffrins may try to kill me. And I don't plan to come back here as a ghost to take tea with you again. So I need the weapons you can get me, and I suggest you think about bodyguards from this point on."

Resi's eyes squinted shut momentarily from an inward pain causing sweat to line his brow. He watched his cigar slowly burning out in the pewter ashtray before him.

"I'll do this for you," the Magister said, appraising Resi more carefully, like he was something expensive he was about to buy. "I'll let you speak with Mr. Ebos. He's in my employ and handles the matters of interest to you. I'll leave everything to him regarding this. You know all firearms are banned in Holland since the mid-century."

"Thank you. And I'll also need a new laptop to use, the most highly powered one you can find. Mine was tampered with and reconfigured in my hotel room, probably courtesy of Jeffrins. He also appropriated my cell phone."

"You certainly had a rough go," the Magister said. With a pained look he picked up a phone on his desk and made a short call in Dutch which Resi didn't understand. Having concluded the call, the Magister sadly shook his head while relighting his own cigar and trying to puff with gusto again, saying, "He'll be on his way shortly with what you need. In the meantime why don't you finish that tea?"

"All right…"

Despite himself, during the interval of waiting, Resi was all but lulled into a somnolent regard again of his opulent surroundings. The antiques had a medicinal effect on his ruffled sensibility and he absently catalogued them in his mind while window shopping. There were period paintings on the wall – even an original Jan Steen, declared the Magister with pride – along with splendid knick-knacks from Amsterdam's maritime heritage. It was a far cry from the rooms and bars he'd seen belonging to Sam Jeffrins along Canal Street. They belonged to a different tradition and were part of the seafaring port city, a part gamily sordid in its blunt reality.

True, all cities had their good and bad sides, of course, but the manners of civic and legal leaders, with all the hypocrisies power necessitated, differed in each; and Amsterdam in the Voorburgwal district was where blinds were left open, even when drawn. Somehow, Resi was equating whatever past innocence he'd lost in his student days with the zealous energies of experience that would constructively brew there, perhaps, before he'd find his absolution.

The Magister had seen something of the ex-Catholic altar boy in him and the fact that Resi was trading paranormal investigative tools for guns visibly displeased the old man.

But Resi wasn't in over his head. Not yet.

The Magister had been watching him through this interim of aesthetic reverie and pointed with his cigar to an ornate silver drinking cup that occupied a nearby bureau, next to a wine glass. "That's a beauty, isn't it? From the 17th century, after the school of Adam van Vianen. Look at it! It's a masterwork of the Baroque era, a rococo extravagance. Look at how the human and animal forms seem to intermingle so as to become almost indistinguishable. The figures…? They're of Venus, Bacchus, Cupid and Ceres! All in a convoluted glitter of ecstasy, yes? It's my Cup of Love, Resi, rarely drunk from, except on special occasions.

Believe me, it's precious, even the Rijksmuseum would pay dearly for it."

The Magister rose to marvel at the glass-enclosed heirloom with its fantastic design celebrating some mythological orgy more like war than love. Having finished his short oration, with cigar in mouth he removed the antique drinking cup from its cabinet – carefully wiping its scalloped interior with a pristine kerchief – and proceeded to fill it with French wine from a vintage bottle he'd uncorked. Drinking deeply from it, still standing, his eyes clouded over with a profound sensual gratification as the libation took effect. For some time he stood holding the silver cup at arm's length and marveling with great astonishment at it.

"Now you must drink," he said finally, extending the cup in a ritual fashion to his still sitting guest.

"No thanks," Resi replied, having watched it all with his unblinking, pale blue eyes. "I've got a hangover, remember?"

"Drink it," the Magister ordered firmly, an unmasked anger on his features, "or you will not see Mr. Ebos at all."

Resi sighed, taking the silver vessel from the old man's liver-pocked hands, feeling its cool and not unpleasant weight within his own palms. For a moment he studied the cup's elaborate figural design on the molding around its border. The sloping part he placed against his mouth to drink a short sip from. Resi let the wine rise over his tongue before handing the cup back to its proud owner.

"There! That wasn't so bad at all," declared the Magister, and finished consuming the wine with a long swallow which moved his Adam's apple up and down a no longer lily white throat. There was a knock on the door as the Magister, with still ceremonial regard, placed the empty cup on the desk.

The Magister bade whoever it was to enter and Resi turned to watch a tall, prepossessing figure come into the stately room. Obviously Dutch, the figure of Velmer Ebos was dressed befitting one hard-working man accustomed to the sea and the outdoors. He wore boots, canvas jacket and camouflage trousers. Ebos removed his cap with the air of one who spends little time inside places like this. Still for such a garb he was no bumpkin, Resi could tell, knowing a true Amsterdam sort when he saw one.

"Velmer, this young man is Mr. Carlton Resi, he's working for me on a possibly dangerous project. I'd like him to be armed with whatever you see fit, pistols and the like. I'm leaving this matter entirely to your discretion, Velmer. Please see that it's immediately accomplished, without any legal complications."

"Yes sir."

The old man smiled as his gloved hand was warmly shaken by Resi before leaving. "I must find some other partner for my games, don't you think?" To Resi it seemed a cryptic remark. He nodded his head deferentially to the Magister, whose attention was immediately on other affairs, judging by the papers he now regarded on his desk. Turning to follow the gruff Ebos out the door, Resi knew he would never again have a tea like the one he'd just been subjected to.

"He's lying to you," Ebos said, once they were in his van grinding a swerving route through the streets. "The Magister doesn't entrust me with anything usually, but I basically do what he wants. Occasionally we screw off on him and he knows it. But pretending to be wrapped up in his courtly and isolated pleasures, he acts like he doesn't understand or see it. He's devious in every matter, to everyone, even the police."

"Oh, wow, is that so?"

Ebos might not have heard. Engrossed in his own driving, he continued: "I'm going to let you decide what you want yourself. You're capable of selecting firearms, aren't you, sir?"

Resi didn't appreciate the man's testiness, but realized he was in the real world again and considered speaking more tactfully. Perhaps he'd behaved badly before the Magister, overwhelmed by the showy conviviality.

"Can you get the kind of guns I want, Ebos?"

"Absolutely, whatever you need, but you may have to return for them...But really, I don't see *why* he's treating you like an oddball American. I don't see it at all."

It was another slight, Resi decided, tired of defending himself.

"He plays too many games. It isn't good. By the way, my friend, you look like you should see a doctor."

"I don't think I'm that wrecked just yet," Resi laughed nervously. "Just a little tired."

"If you're not careful, soon, they won't let you get out of this city. What's it all about?"

"Well." Resi sighed, vaguely noting at street corners all the pedestrians who navigated a welter of traffic. "I don't think I could get out now anyway. I'm back inside a time warp where some things change and others never will."

"You're on drugs?"

"No." Resi didn't laugh now. "I don't know what I'm on. I could tell you the facts, but they're as much a lie, anyway, as anything else. It's all fantastic until it becomes your everyday world, in which case it's everyday stuff. It's basically just a distortion in our recollected reality of all that's past, which has the future in mind. A mistake in galactic physics for the layman..."

"You don't have to talk like that, do you?"

Resi didn't crack a smile this time, sensing the anger. "Okay, I won't. People think a doctor's the right cure, but he's just a supervisor of disease. There's a disease from other creatures down on Canal Street. Maybe I've been infected by it like a young person who deserved better was. Possibly that's why I'm back. I don't know enough about the disease. You want to hear crazy words or something, don't you? That's what you're getting and will continue to get, as long as you humor me and play along."

Ebos shifted through gears, his lips becoming paler. "So

there's a *disease*? And you think the Magister's people carry it? But that disease is normal here. No doctor is needed."

"Is that right? Well, my lady Muse tells me otherwise. Murder has given her an eternal life and she haunts your canals. You should look for her some nights. She whispers things in my ears, better things than your prostitutes do."

Almost too suddenly Ebos stopped the van on Jodenbreestraat, still not looking at Resi as he spoke. "Perhaps you are crazy...But we'll get you some guns now."

# Chapter 5

# In the Spirit of Tau Ceti

"You knew...Laira McKinney?"

Resi nodded to the blowsy, yet still somewhat winsome, female clerk of youthfully indeterminate age. He had come to the Artists and Writers book store near Leidse plein on the rainiest of his days so far in Holland. He had come because the rare book of Laira McKinney's first edition poems bore the address of this small and cozily cluttered store he was wetly standing in, having searched for it with some difficulty while wondering if it still existed.

To his amazement it did. The brusque English clerk, her hair tied in a severe blondish bun, took little notice of the customer who browsed at the wares around him like a man reading tombstone inscriptions. After drying off, he approached the clerk with the volume – a book already his, inscribed to him by the author – which the clerk mistakenly appraised for a moment as another item to ring up.

"Where did you get this?"

"From her," Resi said, relaxing now that her manner had become friendlier and not so business-like. "From Laira McKinney some several years ago; when I was a student here. It's mine as you can see, but she said, if this shop was still here, to show it to Jane Dawson. Is that right...? *Jane Dawson?*"

Resi had done his homework in the Magister's magnificent library. He had scoured microfilm, watched video, read a ton of printed and digital matters until his eyes watered. Copious notes were taken regarding the history of the brief Alien War in Holland around the middle of the 21st century; it was a saga he'd never really learned enough about in school, since it basically happened only in Europe. It was an aberrational horror which had finally happened, and the Dutch were the primary victims who, with the military help of American and Russian forces (including a coalition brigade from other European countries), had succeeded in foiling the Tomu infestation. The dignitaries and political leaders of the time included the Magister's father, Rolfe Hals, who was a leading figure in parliament. His hawkish policies advocated total war against the relatively strange creatures that sprouted up like growing mushrooms along the marshy hinterlands and respective beaches. Many people had died outright from close proximity to the Tomu creatures, causing widespread panic throughout Europe and the world, until their presences were violently exterminated. Photos of Rolfe Hals shaking hands with the American president were prominent in many of the articles Resi had Xeroxed during his research.

He had also found some stuff on Laira McKinney, chiefly in literary sources, including some accounts of her recent disappearance in Amsterdam. She was almost notorious in a way, Resi decided, a young poet with a large readership worldwide who gave publicized readings of her work at universities throughout Europe. She was a naturalist of sorts who spearheaded an ecological group, Aura-scope, determined to spur the government – and many influential Dutch corporations – into rebuilding and refurbishing those war-stricken areas of the Netherlands decimated by years of neglect after the conflict. Photos, tapes, video sources and archived web articles abounded of her group's dramatic demonstrations which had made her a controversial, even hated, figure in more conservative circles. Making matters worse were the published denunciations of the genocidal solution to the Tomu infestation of that time, something she argued was indefensibly criminal. "All of it points to some conspiratorial approach to keep the people of the earth from learning more about what once were their galactic neighbors." A quote from her was in one such article Resi had highlighted. "Isn't it all terribly ironic and tragic for humankind?

Just when we finally learn of the factual existence of extraterritorial life from the Alpha Centauri star system, it is forthwith obliterated by our paranoid leaders and war mongers! And now we'll never be sure if any alien life can exist again, even in the Cetus constellation it presumably came from."

Resi wondered if there were some Aura-Scope writings of Laira's in the book store when the clerk said, "Jane owned this shop indeed."

"So I've heard," Resi said hopefully. "Laira said something like that. And she said Jane and her associates would help her get it back into print."

"Is that right?" the clerk said, though skeptically. She studied the inscription (dated Sept. 2, 2082) on the book's frontispiece, and flipped carefully through its pages. "This is a rare enough edition indeed. Are you willing to sell it?"

"Not really. I'd just like to talk with Jane Dawson for a moment."

"Jane Dawson isn't here. She's in London...and doesn't own Artists and Writers any longer."

Resi's face achieved ground zero. A flame hemorrhage burst somewhere behind his pupils, which contracted nonetheless as he continued regarding this thin woman whose neck he wanted to gently wring. Luckily it was hidden by an unattractive woolen muffler.

Ordinarily the clerk would have ended things quickly, regarding it as merely another minor happenstance in her day. Instead, for some reason, after indirectly appraising the crestfallen Resi, she said: "Lendra's here. She's part-owner now, and was with Jane for years. They're sisters."

"Can I see her?"

The clerk consulted a watch, her brow creased in thoughtful concentration. It was a little after 2 p.m. that rainy afternoon, when dazed or storm-battered people like Resi wandered in. At the moment this soggy American was the only customer in the store. She told him she would go and ask Lendra (if she were around) about the matter, though there was no definite promise in her offhand remark.

Resi turned away, wondering. Behind the counter an oval and gilt-fringed mirror showed a face, resembling his, looking unattractively bedraggled. With the aid of a kerchief he wiped his face off, muttering while regarding the uninviting book stacks around him. He never really understood the poetry in the book Laira gave him; it was too abstractly farfetched for him, belonging to the elitist sensibility of academics. There were also intriguing ink illustrations by her and at night, sometimes, over the years, he would stare at these scribbled renderings of fantastic animals and people, drinking as he did so, believing there might be significance in her art.

There were never enough clues. Some of the drawings seemed to depict the Tomu creatures in all their depressingly squishy glory but he couldn't be absolutely sure.

The clerk returned without the book and to Resi's surprise directed him to follow into an adjacent room. There Lendra Dawson – a mature woman with fulsome blonde hair – awaited him.

Resi gave her his hand. "Hello."

"Resi?" she said, lowering fashionable bi-focal glasses to reveal gray eyes which loomed authoritatively before him. "Resi-the-what...?"

"...Carlton Resi."

"Ah. You know I'm Jane's sister, Lendra. Where did you get this book, Resi?"

To Resi the stoutly-built woman encased in a white sweater and skirt looked more Dutch than English.

"From Laira McKinney, of course..."

"Well, yes, Artists and Writers had a publishing tie-in then as an imprint for certain paperbacks. We don't do that any longer. Not enough money in it. But yes...Jane once published Laira

McKinney I'm sure, and she did read here. Sit down."

Resi sat opposite the woman's messy desk. He declined the beverage she offered, watching her prepare a cup for herself, a usually private ritual which today had an audience. "What part of America are you from?"

"California."

"Ah. We're Americans in spirit, more than ever. Jane went to England, leaving me the store. After all this time some things must remain."

Resi suspected her answer was a little pat for someone whose face was a fallen fruitcake from the ovens. Then he wondered why such a cruel metaphor had surfaced in his thoughts, smiling all the while.

"What is it I can do for you? We don't carry any of Laira's books at the moment. They've sold out, unfortunately. You have a rare first edition." The stout woman leaned forward, expressing token enthusiasm as she affirmed, "I know our inventory practically by heart, day to day. Most of everything my sister did as a publisher in those days is gone, alas."

"Sorry to hear that."

"We were visionaries in those days. Jane was more so than myself. We believed in all sorts of political causes for social change. You know what it was like, don't you? We were activists. There was nothing that we thought we couldn't do! That's the marvel. My sister and Laira McKinney, Resi, were two of a kind in that respect. They were inseparable kindred spirits." A mirthful utterance escaped her then, "And perhaps indecently so! You recall how permissive the era was?" The bespectacled Englishwoman clasped her flat, white, wrinkled hands together reverently, thrilled visibly by remembrance. "It was the age of bohemians with a message of love without enslavement! Of organized resistance to the political oppression as well...Of all of that! And Laira, what has happened to her? We've heard and read horrible things of late."

"I don't know, Miss. Dawson, but I'm hoping to find out."

"Laira back then was an untamed energy. Perhaps it was her rare genius to still be like that to this day." The woman sipped from her cup, eyeing the nervous visitor who kept looking down at the closed book of poetry in his lap. "You're not fully aware of what happened to her?"

Resi coughed, scratching his chin and deciding to reluctantly tell her about his investigation. "I'm doing my best as a private investigator to find out what happened to her and where she might be. Anything you might tell me could be helpful, such as if you know of anyone else who knew her, then or now?"

"Jane of course knows more about her than I ever will. But...you do remember her *accident* some years back, don't you? I'm sure you might suspect it was a backlash connected to her controversial involvement with some unsavory individuals." She chuckled ruefully, doubtless having decried this matter long enough without having a willing ear to tell it to. "That was a time of unusual happenstances, and Laira succumbed to one – almost *fatally* – after immersing herself in a canal in the wretched red-light district of town. At any rate, she was found unconscious and nearly drowned in such muck! I'm not one for untoward speculation but since she was found in such a state, surely it wasn't of her own doing? She wasn't on drugs or anything at that time, though she had been. Someone had to have pushed her in, despite the suicidal impulses we're all heir to now and then. It happened some years back, of course..."

Now Lendra Dawson leaned back, allowing herself a slowly composed smile as she lowered the cup from her rouged lips, savoring the details she'd uttered and how Resi reacted. Again she sighed, gazing around the office which reminded Resi of an elementary school cloakroom clustered with scholarly detritus. At least the place was well-heated and calming to the point where such revelations came easily, for all Laira's past mistakes were in a sense forgiven in the cleansing light of memory.

"Laira had gone beyond the normal bounds, Resi, that's all there is to it. She was in the Nietzsche-like immorality of unrestrained thought. She, who had preached the politics of poetry as a cosmic love to come, for all creatures from whatever origin, spread her body, mind, and soul around like there was no tomorrow and berated everyone day and night about the world's evils, which only Aura-Scope could vanquish. Surely, yes, we remember her, it was only yesterday...! She was a very complex and talented poet who should have stayed in her own neck of the woods. Her misfortune was to stray from there."

"Miss. Dawson, if it wasn't just an accident, who would have pushed her in?"

"I don't know, not specifically. If she were in her right mind, maybe it would never have happened, her high profile to the world would have remained. She used to hang around that nightclub, the Hyperion, nearby here. That wild place for people doing what they do and always have done, letting their minds and bodies go to hell...Now she might be one of the great social martyrs after all," Lendra Dawson scoffed, defensively crossing her arms. "Oh yes. A Lorelei of these waterways, haunting them, you're telling me? More rubbish for demented minds reading beer labels and not literature...The more Laira found out what the world was like, the greater her frustration, the more she could not accept or deal with it. The more she had to escape into a transcendent realm of rebellion, her 'hiding place'...and it's as simple as that, Resi. Also, the people she was with were vermin, unspeakably so."

*But I'm not,* Resi's eyes said, still immersed in unfathomable desperation.

"Miss. Dawson...about these people she knew. The ones you're talking about. Can you remember some by name? Can you tell me something about one named Van Groot, a local businessman, or about Sam Jeffrins, who once knew Laira?" The fire behind his pupils was a night flare, Resi knew that much.

"Did *you* know him?"

The Dawson woman shook her head vehemently, but Resi felt he detected a sign of recognition on her face regarding this name anyway. He persisted now in questioning her, but she continued shaking her head with a look that said it was getting late in the afternoon.

At that moment another husky woman wearing a voluminous blue dress appeared from the store's shadowy recesses and surprised them, saying, "Because you've been investigating diligently Laira's plight, I think you deserve to know more of the facts. I just returned from London a little while ago…I'm Jane."

It was indeed Jane Dawson introducing herself, Resi knew. Her bold hazel eyes burned unwaveringly back at him. To Resi she might well be a fairy goddess in the rotund flesh, making her appearance in the underground reality show his life had become. Why he now saw her as such he had not the time nor will to ponder.

"Did you know a UFO once landed in Leiden, an undetermined time ago and only the Nazis knew of it?"

"Jane!" Lendra tried to caution. She held up a gnarled forefinger in warning.

"Only a select few Nazis knew of it actually, Mr. Resi, way back in the waning days of World War II. And of course it became an extremely classified secret." With a ponderous motion of her feet in their brown slippers she edged closer to Resi. Her advancing presence was a command to be critically listened too–then believed.

## Chapter 6

# All Truth Seekers Hear the Vibrato Chord

"Laira's great grandmother, Kendra was apparently the only Dutch person to view the landing. According to the account given by the Nazis, known only by a few to this day, she was abducted and taken inside the oblong craft by the Tomu visitors."

Jane poured herself a large cup of English tea as she spoke, still measuring Resi. (*Not another tea service,* he thought.)

"I'll spare you the exact details since you only need to know the general facts. You know the Nazis were keenly interested in the occult, all the black arts plus missile technologies, secret weapons and what have you. They may have had collusion with the Tomu beings on that craft, or even have summoned it through their dark machinations...Laira is not actually dead or alive as we speak. She exists in an in-between state, a cryptic gap in time-space from which she plays her game of hide-and-seek with us, and everybody else."

The shocked expression on Resi's mug easily exceeded a thousand digital words to describe it. "I never expected this," he stammered. "How did you know about her and all this?"

"You've asked for it, and I'm thankful to know what you're up to. You have certainly risked your welfare for it."

Lendra sat shaking her head and in her dismay knocked over a jug of milk, which slowly formed a puddle on the Oriental rug. She was in no hurry to clean it up.

"I can only tell you Laira McKinney's family has been cursed since that terrible day her great grandmother was abducted, then subsequently experimented on, either by those non-humans or the Nazis...perhaps together. They were not just trying to create a master Aryan race – they were also diligently creating a race of hybrid slaves to do their nefarious bidding. Even the Tomu would use such slaves for their own purposes from the planet they came from. Then, many years later, Laira's own mother was abducted as well, decades after the Alien War. So we know they have come and gone again; Laira even has photographic proof of her mother's abduction, which took place just a few years before her own. What happened to Laira occurred because she came here needing my assistance and wherewithal to begin her investigation into her mother's disappearance and the history of her family abductions, in all innocence, hoping to find answers to why this curse so bedevils the McKinney maternal lineage. I of course have helped her, as I'm prepared to help you, though I should warn this, all could have irreparably grave consequences for all of us."

*Bingo,* Resi thought, actually accepting his tea now with gusto. Bring on the green gooey mothers! He was strangely without fear and his viral malaise lifted the more he discovered genuine facts about the case.

"But she shouldn't have involved Jane and me in all this, despite what you think, she shouldn't have used her countercultural connections to serve her private ends," declared Lendra, still absently regarding the milk puddle. "She was warned by us to stay away from both parties, yet she wouldn't heed advice. She became involved, as I've told you, with despicable individuals who used her for their own gain."

"Don't confuse the gentleman, Lendra. We are as much activists in our own right, supporting Laira McKinney's causes, which were political in some respects, to this day."

"Where is she? What really happened to her?" Resi demanded, rising from his chair.

"That I can't exactly tell you, Mr. Resi, except she's not of this world and probably will never be again. Not in the flesh as we know it. The secret of her fate lies in a classified location even your Magister has sought to know, and bringing you to our town explains it. You'll know in due time, when an ally of ours contacts you, but I have to ask you this: Will you serve our cause or betray us?"

"What do you mean? I only want to find what's truly happened to Laira."

"She has told us where she is in her own way. To learn that and other things you'll have secrets to keep for us, understand? Your Magister will have to be left in the dark in certain matters."

"You don't trust him..."

"It could possibly endanger many of us, just when we've succeeded in protecting ourselves for so long from that Sam Jeffrins..."

"And from that awful Hotel Nieuw crowd," Lendra sullenly chimed in.

"You would only make trouble for everyone if you continued your unusual investigation on your own, Mr. Resi, I'm sure."

"I'm quite willing to cooperate with your partner, Miss Dawson. Be assured of it, whatever it takes, even if it means serving two masters."

Jane Dawson snorted and sipped her tea, having regally seated herself in a filigreed chair next to Lendra. Her granny glasses nearly glowed phosphorescently, despite the low-wattage table lamp, crested by a 17th century naked putto blowing a ceramic trumpet.

"As long as you don't serve the galactic Satan, I can only advise you not to become too personally involved in all this. I don't remember you from those years back when you knew Laira, but she told me a little about you."

"I can't help having certain character faults," Resi admitted. "You know there's something in the Nieuw, an energy affecting me to whatever good or bad end. I feel like I even know Laira intimately again."

"That energy you speak of is like something possessing Laira as well, which you're doubtlessly suffering the backlash of. It seeks to exploit your senses in a derogatory way you'll have little control over if you're not careful."

Lendra nodded her head at her sister's remark. "It will bring out the devil," she concurred. "Maybe even the Tomu."

To say the least, Resi knew. He was pacing about the secluded storage area he later found, realizing the Dawson sisters were his only means to find out more and they were obviously not fond of the Magister, who was a charlatan to them. One connected also to that sinister business world they wanted no part of. "This energy you're talking about. Is it supernatural or extraterrestrial?" Resi had asked. He was in a ticklish bind, since his devices weren't geared to the latter.

Jane Dawson's guttural voice remained adamant. Whatever produced "the vicious vibrato" was what the Nazis had sought desperately to exploit as a weapon in the war's final years. It would also be valuable now to the repugnant likes of Sam Jeffrins, who could sell its digital components to international terrorists. It was better leaving such a thing to the heavens rather than human beings, Resi knew. Yet he couldn't refrain from asking too many questions of the Dawson sisters. Did such a mysterious energy entity have a language perhaps, one he could use to communicate with Laira's spirit at the secret location, if indeed she were there and not residually still at the Nieuw?

"I advise you not to go poking around that hotel anymore, Resi. You know they're aware you're up to something there. If you cross a line you know what the consequences could be," Jane Dawson finished, setting her tea cup down. Switching her attention to her still morose sister she said, "Please clean up the mess you've made, Lendra. Or let the cats do it."

Resi's vibrato chord connected him to an unknown central operating system he was sure existed, partly as a doubtless underworld cell, at the Hotel Nieuw. How long it had been there was anyone's guess. One thing was certain: somehow the vibrating emanations had infected him, nestled inside his brain like a parasitic nemesis holding him in thrall to the pain game.

He knew now Jeffrins was pushing the buttons – but for who? Turncoat Jeffrins was a mercenary and a terrorist accomplice who flourished in the underdeveloped parts of Holland ravaged by the Alien War of long ago. In some ways Jeffrins' brand of mercenary terrorism was directed at select individuals who became the means for promoting a proliferating global exploitation scheme backed by black market weapons.

Laira McKinney was one of his means, dead or alive. He was pursuing her again in the spirit world as he had once in the corporeal one and Resi wondered if the black marketer somehow contributed to her fate by possibly being in connection with the Tomu aliens who supposedly once abducted her. Or maybe Jeffrins was planning to deny them access to her; she was that important to the aliens if they had the ability to make earthly contact again, just as Laira's great grandmother had been.

But who had hacked into his computer if not Jeffrins, incredible as it seemed. It initiated the streaming viral chord Resi was at first unconscious of, until time whirled its cogs and he realized what the thralldom of terror really was.

Other individuals were in thralldom as well throughout Europe – Resi was sure of it. Sam Jeffrins was an underground operative of base pursuits attempting to use those like Resi for his own pernicious ends. Resi knew he was supposed to document it all as, The Para Eye, the world knew him to be, to convey a misleading propaganda and prove whatever needed proving in keeping the curious at bay. In time everyone would know what the basis for the incipient terror was, like an ultimatum that had to be taken seriously, no matter what, no matter how the alien dogs of war bayed.

The answer he assured himself was to temporarily deactivate his laptop. It was a pulsing and improvised explosive device now.

Could he replace its hijacked operating system with his own? Ironically he had used his PC hardly at all since arriving in Amsterdam, especially after conjecturing it had been tampered with by someone, or some force, who deliberately reconfigured it for him in his hotel room. Resi was surprised to find it still existed, for he was sure it was an item Jeffrins had taken along with his cell phone. Or maybe it had simply been switched with another incredibly resembling his? Now, in one of the internet cafes nearby the Dam, Resi had the silver notebook back on, and realized he was taking a proverbial chance booting up to a link he wanted contained. He wasn't even sure the damn thing still worked after what had happened. He needed a hot spot, for it no longer automatically connected him to the net from anywhere in the world.

The image on his laptop screen greeting Resi nearly knocked him over. Internal coded warning messages were multiplying into red pixels without meaning, all accompanied by a vibrating hiss. Sitting next to him a bearded Dutch university student openly marveled at the digital spectacle, crying *"Far out!"* as he rose to leave the table. In the café's excited chatter the student's amazed remarks had trouble finding their way to Resi's chapped ears.

*All political prisoners of the state will go to Maze Niner,* a strident female voice announced, imploding aurally now as another command might in Resi's psyche. The voice repeated the message with the impersonal coldness of a cell phone's automated voice announcing the time.

The white snow on his computer screen slowly dissolved the conflicting colored specks into a rather beautiful female face, one both familiar and strange. It was rainbow-hued and frosty with digital distortion. *I will take you to Maze Niner and have designated a meeting place for us. Make sure you're there,* the facial vision advised as if looking into the remnants of Resi's body and outmoded soul.

Before leaving he checked his watch and consulted a small spiral notebook he kept to jot down the specifics, and also to try and contain his nerves. He was becoming a jittery mass of neurons again, controlled by that female face in his machine, he was sure.

Out in the street, as always, Resi was walking into the night with all its possibly hostile elements, he dodged a few impatient bicyclists. Leonardo da Vinci once wrote that the eye was the window to the soul, but Resi knew he was going blind, that someone had broken the window on his computer screen – and there was no way to fix it.

# Chapter 7

# The Hidden Tablet

In the deadfall of winter's pall, there he was, pacing by store windows in the Spuii district. Freezing, unshaven, wondering if fate had reserved a place for him in a pantheon in hell, Carlton Resi smoked another unfiltered cigarette and, with obvious discontent, ceaselessly kept checking his watch. Where was the mysterious cyber-witch?

The mere sight finally of Ms. Zu was more frightening to Resi than a boatload of snakes in the Amazon wild. She was a tall young woman, an oriental beauty without question, dressed like a dominatrix who had stepped out of a chic torture chamber. Wearing a long black overcoat with upturned mauve collar, blue spandex gloves, and lace-up boots with spiky heels, she approached Resi and demurely asked, "Have you been standing out here looking lost, without a hot drink, expecting me?" Her voice to Resi smacked of an unmusical radio whine his ears recoiled from. "Just call me Zu, please."

"Glad we're past the amenities."

"Way past." She tightened the billowing red scarf around her neck. Rudeness became her, Resi thought. "To quell any curiosity, it would be better if at this point you don't want to know more than Jane might have told you, about me or anything for that matter, okay?"

"Not even the Maze?"

"Not even that."

"Are you Dutch?"

"I'm a British citizen, but I've spent many years in Holland…Enough? And we won't discuss Laira McKinney at the moment."

They were slowly meandering along outside some coffee store

vicinity when Resi, indicating his tote bag, asked her in blunt fashion how she had invaded his computer?

"I negotiated obstacles at the Hotel Nieuw. Bribing the clerk allowed me to find where you were. I commend you on your utter secrecy, since this isn't the first time your PC has been tampered with. When you were out of it I entered your room and adjusted your laptop. But I was hoping to find you there. I actually needed to find out what was in there causing your reported dysfunction."

"You mean my sick and quirky actions?"

"Exactly, Resi...Don't you feel better? That hotel room reeked of something your bodily system didn't acclimate for sure."

"Yeah, it was like a slow burn radiation poisoning from cyberland. Thanks, I guess."

They were in front of a small shop now, very quaint-looking with a few electronic tablets in its display window, surmounted by a neon sign which blinked the red word "SPLANX" continuously. It occurred vaguely to Resi he'd seen this shop before, or one like it, upon arriving in Amsterdam. The tablets had caught his eye because of their unusual look and the advertisement proclaiming them to be 'a futuristic cure for the present,' with an emblazoned spaceship logo as well. There were avenues of a great city like this to get lost on and Resi found his cogitation stopped by Zu's forceful hand on his back.

"We have to get inside, man."

"Even if it's closed, which it looks to be?"

"Absolutely...This is our best chance and they don't come easy."

"That's what *she* said."

"I didn't find this place overnight. The owner keeps moving around. It took some doing and luck."

"What are we looking for?"

"A tech geek entrepreneur named Hiram de Hazeraux... Probably a lame alias."

Luckily the shop and its street were in a typically narrow alley of what Resi called a cobblestone quietus. But the tremors in his paranoid psyche returned now louder and more active than usual as they appraised the building. The side door naturally was their best bet, looking so woodenly fragile. With a pointy tool Zu quickly had the door lock sprung to allow access. They entered as discreetly as a pair of nouveau burglars might.

Inside it was total darkness and Resi raked his shin on a crate or something before Zu found a light switch. They were in a back storeroom now, one that had previously been visited by an unwelcome guest no doubt, for the place was ransacked to say the least. There were scattered pools of blood they nearly slipped over in, adding to the gagging stench of flesh decaying in a bad butcher shop. But no one was about, especially one Hiram de Hazeraux or his body. Only a radio was on, playing oldie Dutch popular songs accentuating the eerie surroundings.

To Zu it all didn't look good, and she began searching through the rubble after putting a found blood sample into a small vial.

"It's incredibly cold in here," Resi noted. "It's worse than outside. Do you feel that blast of cold air?"

Zu nodded and produced a small pistol that wasn't a surprise to Resi. Her eyes evolved into icy slits peering into every dusty cranny. Resi meanwhile held up an EMF detector he scanned the room with, especially near a cold radiator.

"I'm already getting spikes. There's something here, the meter's really jumping."

"What's that supposed to do?"

"It's searching for any spirit presence here. This is probably a crime scene."

Zu nodded, knowing this was one good reason to have Resi along, among possibly others. A murdering spirit seemed outlandish, or maybe it had witnessed something unspeakable they needed to know about. The chill was increasing, causing her teeth to uncontrollably chatter. Zu ignored Resi's wanting to leave, if only for her own sake, and just then, behind the radiator on the musty, frigid floor, Resi found something. It glowed like an otherworldly presence.

"Jesus, Zu, look at this…"

It was like being back in the hotel room where Laira McKinney had been mind-raped and abused repeatedly until, well, her eventual scarifying end according to the book store sisters. And here they were in another strange store, with the occupant either missing or dead. Were these all facts or just misleading fallacies leading them in a deceptive vicious circle, Resi wondered.

"That's unbelievable," Zu said, examining the diamond tablet in her gloved hands. She held it like one would a holy grail. "It's *his* tablet, Resi. *His* Splanx, I think. Look how it scrolls his name across the screen." She let out an accompanying murmur of disbelief, staring back at his incredulous eyes. "If Jeffrins was here, he certainly overlooked what he wanted the most."

"How could he? This place has been thoroughly turned over."

"Where on earth was it hidden?"

Zu peered behind the radiator and surmised the tablet had been wedged inside a wall compartment, partially ajar, until Resi extricated it. Resi half-marveled at the workings of fate, but abruptly his detector spiked again and he felt *the thing's* presence. A monstrous presence, like one never felt before, uttering a low sibilant vibrato his ears registered while goose bumps sprouted into pinpoints on his arms and elsewhere. "It's still here," he told her, the concern in his voice beyond amber alert.

"Where is it?" Zu asked, still seeing only the store room's disheveled confines. Then she screamed, startling Resi into nearly dropping his detector – along with the prized tablet – and, staggering, they both lunged towards the door. "Something has bitten or scratched me!" she wailed at him as Resi tried to push her from the area. Knowing what that meant, hearing the growl grow menacingly as he did so; the thing's blurred outline became a mammoth shape changer which, for a moment, resembled a gelatinous creature long believed extirpated from the earth's face, until now. In its energy manifestation it thankfully ebbed as they made it out of the store room and back into the drizzly street.

"You'll be okay," Resi tried reassuring her, both of them out of breath.

"Have you got the tablet?" Zu kept saying, her voice finally drained of the fear which had possessed them. "I dropped my gun back there…"

Forget it, Resi wanted to tell her, he was about to score enough firearms for both of them. Still he wondered about the imminent arrival of the police. Resi and Zu had left something awful, yes, but was it actually a crime scene involving the unorthodox Doctor de Hazeraux? What if the blood was animal – or *alien*— instead of human, and de Hazeraux himself returned later to see what his shop had been turned into by his otherworldly pet? Anything good or bad was possible, he knew, but at this point how much either mattered escaped him. Resi knew something perhaps paranormal and dangerous lurked in this little shop in Amsterdam and he was willing to believe anything now.

Resi would soon be looking up into the night sky towards the southeast in the Cetus constellation. The Dawson sisters told him of a star called Tau Ceti that was about twelve light years from the earth. It had been hallowed in the annals of science fiction, and maybe soon in science fact even more. Five planets were supposed to be known to be around that star, with one planet in the habitable zone having a mass five times that of earth. Maybe that one planet was where the Tomu alien race had come from, just another curious cliché in a known lore once predictable as sitcom television in an earlier age?

# Part II

Maze Niner

# Chapter 8

# Into Leonardo's Closet of Mirrors

Eventually Resi was sponging down Zu's wound in the privacy of her well-heated flat, a temporary headquarters for her no doubt. He carefully reassured Zu that her back, though scratched, wasn't as beet red as she feared.

"It really hurt there for a minute," she admitted, showing an unguarded vulnerable side for the first time. "You say you saw the apparition?" Her hands were whiter than ever, clenching the large green bath towel she pressed against her chest. Resi wondered how he kept getting into such ticklish predicaments, though somewhat enjoying this one. Lady Zu was as much woman as witch, it appeared – perhaps more so.

"I saw its outline for a moment as it tried to manifest fully, but somehow it didn't – or couldn't, and my detector went stone dead."

"It was bestial. What do you think it was?"

"Something paranormal, but perhaps not of this earthly creation...I've never dealt with an animal or creature's spirit before, only ghostly humans. The good news of course is it's dead, it has to be, since my detector picked it up like any other spirit mass. The bad news is that it may have the power to completely manifest and hurt others the way it did you. It was huge, at least ten feet tall."

Zu muttered and shook her head, pulling her blouse back on and slowly buttoning it. She wore no bra and her breasts through the sheer fabric stood out enough for Resi to marvel. "We have to get going," she said. "There's more to this than I thought. We have to find de Hazeraux before the police get involved in this and limit our alternatives. Also the winter's closing in, which means bad weather into the bargain."

"Shouldn't you have a doctor check that? I mean it was caused by something we have no idea as to whether it's infectious or not..."

"Not at the moment. We've got to get moving before your friend Jeffrins gets a bead on us." She moved to a coffee table where the SPLANX was, picking up the tablet and critically regarding it again. "I've got to get the blood samples and this checked out by our tech specialist pronto if possible, that might take a few hours. I'm afraid to fool with it on my own."

"Good idea," Resi agreed. "In the meantime, I've got to pick up a few necessary items promised me by the Magister, at his place outside the city. I think we'll definitely be needing protection and a lot more."

She handed him one of her prized cell phones and said, "We'll need to keep in touch. Bring your computer as well. I'm lending you my Peugeot, the black one you see parked on the street outside."

Peeking through a wrinkled curtain window at the street below, Resi whistled appreciatively as he appraised the vehicle. He was good to go.

"Won't you need it too?"

"Not until you get back. So please make sure it remains in good condition. We're probably going to put some miles on it soon. If not I have a back-up."

"How did a girl like you get into something like this, Zu, if you don't mind my asking?"

"I told you not to get inquisitive, didn't I?"

"I have the feeling you once knew Laira McKinney just as I did. I forgot to ask if you knew anything about that little boy I encountered at the door of her old room at the Hotel Nieuw? She was supposed to hang out there a lot once, when Jeffrins had a grip on her. Bad things happened there."

Putting on her overcoat Zu looked again at Resi and sighed. "A pretty little fat boy with carrot top hair, right...? She had a son, you know, though it wasn't well known. It was something she kept as secretive as everything else in her misguided life. Whether he is really biologically hers I don't know."

Resi's mouth had partially dropped open in surprise. "A son...? Who was his father?"

Zu shook her head again, brushing back long strands of jet black hair from her eyes. She put the SPLANX carefully inside her tote and zipped it up. "I know you'll find that out for both of us," she said. Lightly tinted green glasses were now affixed to her face and Rooksana Zu's manner was professional again. "Make sure you call me on that phone once an hour for a status check, even if you just text me."

In Resi's consciousness the *grachtenhuizen* became a brown and sandwiched together wall of gabled rooftops as he drove by. All those 16th century gables passed before his eyes, revealing their evolution through the winter scarred ages, so many wooden rooftops frayed by the elements. There were curving necked bell gables that had replaced the conventional step or spout types here and there, finally culminating in the rather polished French cornices.

In this shifting panorama the ages and their gables appeared to merge and interact, bastardizing the fine lines of time and demarcating one another. Carlton Resi perceived the eternal Bosch-like phantasmagoria his experience of this European culture and its architecture had become. In his imagination alien beasts hung from the gables (or stood atop them with circus-like bravado), mocking him with their contortions, sporting flagrant and bizarre tails with corpuscular variation, all beckoning to him to admit the folly of his mundane quest and somehow join them.

Resi refused, instead driving slowly by the houses lining the canals, debating when to leave the city. He would not join the imaginary parade above him, where the monsters and men cavorted in indecent display, and naked women were imprisoned in stocks and rusting chains. He yearned to call Zu and inform her of all this. He would not attempt to climb the building sides like a skillful ape and scale those rooftops where the historic panoply of time and circumstance played itself out. Instead Carlton Resi would continue to drive through the crepuscular weather, seemingly painted by time and nature's merciless hand, desiring confrontation with his fate yet simultaneously fighting it.

He was being drawn back to the Hotel Nieuw, and there was nothing he could do about it. On the shotgun seat his laptop was open and similar unspeakable images flashed across the screen. Why couldn't he just pitch it out the window and be done with it. Were they all trying to do him in via this device of devious emanations?

On his route through this stream dream of history he mentally pitched, stumbled, until he was no longer in one age but all ages to come. All the ages conflicted within him, yet none was more dominant than the other. Was that equality or anarchy? Resi in his temporal inebriation could not determine the answer. The emanation had hijacked him via the cyber-link again, overriding all that Zu had probably reconfigured into it. How was that possible? On he drove, until the entire city seemed one connected street encompassing all the designs of hell. On he drove, passing through what had once been a Jewish ghetto, now razed, except in memory and monuments. He was tired – quite tired – and felt like he might die in this section, corroded like a menorah left unlit too long, in Jodenbuurt.

Then he turned around, heading back to the damnable hotel, hearing Laira's chanting voice. He left the computer and the car in a nearby parking garage, taking only the phone with him. It was a repetitive process he was becoming all too familiar with, finally he reached the building he knew both their rooms would be forever at. How he managed to again navigate the torturously steep stairs he couldn't understand. All he would ever really recall was the room's merciful ambience, with him lying spread-eagled on its low, hard bed. In the eternity of that rest he sought to withdraw from his stupor – his hopelessness – but was unable to. *She was there.* She was a presence more felt than clearly discerned in the room's musty dimness. Laira McKinney was there, demurely sitting in an old chair by the curtained windows, and her voice had gained a quiet but articulate resonance within his head, vying with the vibrato static and what once had been pure, ululating agony. Her voice now was humanly patient, instructing, almost decidedly affectionate, and very British. He recalled the times in this very hotel when her voice transfixed him with its accent and rhythms, producing a profoundly rapturous sensation of aesthetic transcendence. The rest of her was beauty, a moral beauty, incarnate as well.

She was eternally young dressed in her flea market ensemble of retro hippie clothing, aglow with beads and the parti-colored dress with its billowing silk folds. She wore a wide-brimmed lady's hat, festooned by a frontal flower, popular in a bygone century. There in her seat by the curtained window, Laira McKinney could have posed for any old master like Vermeer or Hals, but now she was posing for him. For whatever current flowed river-like through Resi's eyes, bathing all as ablative radiance might. Resi kept staring at her full apparition, trying to perceive and place the vision of her true self absolutely within his consciousness and banishing all else to the inferior waste-lands outside.

They were both in the past, an eternal past in the present. Without fear she rose from the chair and slowly approached his figure on the bed. In a now innocent floating nervousness, Resi waited, child-like, feeling her smooth the nape hairs of his neck, her manner imploring him to do things he had no inkling of. In the moment's sereneness there was still a tension and Resi felt voyeur-like and almost apart from it. He was in the languorous mystery of a mindless trance there was no escaping. In the

SPLANX

evanescent shadows her form pressed against the muscular solidity of his back, lingering there for a breath-drawn instant, before releasing itself when his back failed to relax or accommodate her yearning overture. Her powder blue hat fell as a slow moving wing to the floor. Resi saw the expression of her sorrow which froze into a portrait of immaculate suffering, one borne finely and selflessly. Veins throbbed on a temple unmarred by wrinkling and Resi knew there was something fatal in her spirit's irrevocable being. With that in mind he struggled to regain full consciousness. He managed to weakly sit up on the bed and stare about the room's gray interior. Where had she gone? There was no sign of the boy with red hair either.

Resi picked up his tote, preparing to leave the room and realized he had picked up Zu's at her flat by mistake. They were not off to a good start. Rummaging through it he noted a fully loaded 9mm Beretta pistol with the safety off, which he slipped inside his jacket before leaving the room. How did such an outlawed antique get into Zu's bag, who did the witch really work for, he wondered. It was another oddity in a series of such he hoped to get explanations for. He just hoped the antique worked.

Downstairs in the bar/lobby area he ran into the purported owner, Van Groot, doing some paperwork at his office. The gruff owner was not glad to see Resi of course and didn't look up when greeted. The adjacent bar was closed, its doors bolted and windows shuttered. Van Groot's office window was open and Resi noted it had started to rain outside.

"I'd like to know who has been in my room while I've been out."

"I don't know, people come and go here," Van Groot said.

"Has Sam Jeffrins been around? I hear he used to come here often."

Van Groot made a low humming sound as he consulted a leather bound ledger on the large desk he was sitting at. There

76

wasn't a computer in sight. The office reminded Resi of just another converted hotel room, with hardly expensive furnishings and not well-maintained. The floor was a scuffed wooden once except for ratty throw rugs here and there. Acrid smoke from Van Groot's soggy cigar pervaded the air.

"What kind of building is this really, Van Groot?"

"Why don't you sit down there?" the owner said a shade convivially, indicating a wooden chair nearby while continuing to peruse his paperwork. "It's starting to get rainy now."

Resi repeated his question as Van Groot consulted his ledger, muttering something before looking up again. "You do not have to know," he said calmly, his distant gray eyes now regarding his visitor. "Is there any problem for you? As far as I know, everything's okay. I know you have an association with the Magister. Maybe you should be asking him these things?"

Upstairs on the Nieuw's top floor Sam Jeffrins paced back and forth in the same browbeaten room where Resi had earlier encountered Laira McKinney's spirit. He drank from a whisky flask and cursed his luck. Somehow he felt Resi was learning more about things than he was. It severely pissed him off, considering how he paid people to keep him foremost in the loop on whatever was happening. Resi was being watched like never before, a pigeon they let fly free to hopefully lead them to secret places and people they must discover.

Even more disturbing was the fact they had let the tablet genius Hiram de Hazeraux slip away into parts unknown. It was partially his fault, Jeffrins knew, being asleep at the switch and not staying on top of things. But what he'd seen that night at de Hazeraux's little shop had made him a believer. That tablet the lanky witch doctor used against Jeffrins' men unleashed something terrible when they tried to take it away, causing him to lose a man in the bargain. Jeffrins had never seen anything like the monstrous *Soma* (as the slinky Indian inventor de Hazeraux called it) conjured up to nearly kill them. Jeffrins knew he was lucky to still be functionally alive. It was something he'd never seen before and only wanted to see again when *he* had the power to use it against others, which certainly would happen if what he planned worked out.

When his cell rang Jeffrins was hardly in the mood to answer it.

"I think you should know that American friend of yours, Resi, is back snooping around. I told him I hadn't seen you," a nervous Van Groot said.

"No shit. That's just great...I won't be long here, amigo."

Jeffrins sat down by the window and peered out at the rain cascading downwards outside. He tried to remember Laira McKinney alive. She was unreachable to him then, an enigmatic wraith of a child-woman who was both beautiful and strange. Tall, willowy, with pale blonde hair reaching to her waist, she was an athletic sprite with the best well-muscled female legs Sam Jeffrins had ever seen. And she was a paradox as well – at first glance, anyway, despite all her defensiveness – who wrote poetry he didn't like or understand. Had he known those books she read at the Amsterdam University, he might have detected a Pre-Raphaelite sensibility in her bearing, among other unorthodox traits gleaned from the world of art and fashion. Jeffrins couldn't even understand why he had killed her, how she had pleaded for her life just a few months ago in this very room. Now she was unreachable for everybody, except perhaps for that damn ghost hunter, Resi, of all people, who supposedly had something paranormal going with her. Jeffrins wanted to laugh but was so befuddled by it all he refrained from treating it like a joke. In truth he felt like a dupe, using sick mutants who incompetently misused their infections.

*"A passion for the gods in galaxies beyond as humans we once loved Foreshadows our future again..."*

He could hear her reading those lines to him as if yesterday, lines from her bad and confused poetry. What the hell was it supposed to mean, he thought, to have passion for gods in galaxies beyond? Jeffrins shook his head and took a long pull from the flask. Now she was up there somewhere, floating around like silly putty, only he saw nothing, only the same dismal ceiling above with its mold spots…and the darkening ones below.

From his jacket he extracted a rumpled paperback of Laira's poetry. It bore traces of her dried blood, browner with each day's passing. After he had raped and cut up her naked flesh with his hunting knife, Jeffrins had read portions of her poetry to Laira's dead body. He kept remembering it all now as he tapped the same blade on his knee and noted there was still her blood on the knife as well. They would never find her unless they were capable of draining the North Sea.

"Come on, bitch, let me cut off your ghost titties…"

Again Jeffrins tried reading the blood-drenched pages of her poetry. The lines were from a poem called "My Sister's Late Ecstasy," they perplexed Sam Jeffrins just as Laira McKinney had those times he would watch her lithe movements around the hotel. In this world she was out of place then, even flirting with danger the way she did, hanging around Jeffrins' interests on Canal Street. Who was she? She was a twenty-eight-year-old brat who lived her early years in London and came from a wealthy American family she renounced because it had 'forsaken her humanity.' Yet she had still lived off a parental stipend she claimed to have severed in order to live in the low-life sections of Amsterdam, where the city was trendy, hip, and filled with artistic ferment and a spiritual revivalism. The sad thing to Jeffrins was that Carlton Resi, a homeboy American, had helped her during her transition from bad bar chick to poet rebel.

Jeffrins used her money, along with everything else he could, since in the beginning he functioned as her halfway pimp in a way. He reviled Laira for her naively brash and stupid hypocrisy.

He would teach her a lesson therefore, since she was destined for the city's streets like so many of the young women who toiled for him. That would be her real and ultimate level, despite her breeding, airs, arty talents and intelligence; all that fascinated yet repelled him, all that he had to make her pay dearly for. The price would naturally be extracted from her fine body, which Jeffrins sado-masochistically abused in his fashion. He would demean her to a point where she'd ultimately want to even become his live-in prostitute. There was a crowd of jerks out there who'd gladly pay for Laira's favors. There were many in his bourgeois hierarchy who'd like to spank her faux hippie behind, while Jeffrins enjoyed her humiliation.

From his bastion of voyeuristic visions a young Carlton Resi witnessed many fights between this odd pair of lovers who were also his friends. A part of him was appalled by what Laira had gotten herself into; another part wanted her to become a submissively chastened acolyte of further sexual games he'd be included in. But Laira had called him 'a silly alcoholic sucker' who didn't know what to do with his life. After the university lectures, Resi sat the hours away on his familiar hotel bar stool, dreaming of simple pleasures she called bourgeois, quite apart from the thrilling underground life of political and artistic rebellion she was leading. Along with everything else he was less worldly than Sam Jeffrins, who was trying to woo her away from the bookish life she led at the Artists and Writers book store. It had become a second home to her now, and Jeffrins claimed she'd fallen under the influence of those rotten Dawson lesbian bitches that ran the place: "Sucking up shitty tea while finger fucking each other," was how he'd put it.

Trying to wean Laira away from that cultural den was an unsolvable problem that got the best of Sam Jeffrins now and then. Slapping her delicate and beauteous flesh in a display of virile outrage wasn't the answer. Resi couldn't understand why she took such beatings considering her non-violent beliefs. She was a refined glutton for punishment; black and blue bruises were her equivalent of tattoos. It was something awful to behold, Resi knew. Was this what she deserved for trying to reform the world? To stop turf wars on Canal Street wasn't the brightest thing to do for a collegiate wunderkind who partied with dive bar derelicts like Jeffrins. In a way her pacifist actions in the local bar wars was in homage to the fact Sam Jeffrins was a dark force to be reckoned with, whether in this life or the next and that unwittingly – and perhaps fatally – she'd trespassed into the magnetic field of his influences and become irremediably pinioned there, another rare butterfly species whose wings were bitten off by savages.

They were a threesome: Jeffrins, Laira, and Resi all bound by vagaries of time and friendship which made them alternate seeing things together, pretending to be each other intermittently, so that past times fused with the present while foreshadowing their futures.

Somehow, Resi had enough of it and turned away from them, never wanting to see the hotel room where he made love and hate, never to know of its troubling secrets or admit to anyone what games had been played there. Somehow he had to believe that patriarchal Sam Jeffrins was the toughest and straightest dude alive, unlike the arty wimps mocking the true values Resi wanted to live by. Ironically too, somehow, Laira McKinney was the epitome of female beauty in her way; though prone to a woman's erratic nature, she would never allow herself to become a submissive whore. Only a collegiate lady poet whose body bore the bloody excoriations of a man totally obsessed with her.

They were all young and angry and that's what Carlton Resi marveled at then, traveling one day on the tram through rainy Amsterdam with her book of poetry in his hands. The inscription of its frontispiece read: *"To the Voddenjood...to the 'rag and bones Jew.'"* Still grappling with the puzzle her life and work became to him, Resi's abstract wondering ceased when he realized the tram had passed considerably out of the city, that the scenery glimpsed through the window was a relatively pastoral tableau well beyond his scheduled stop. Looking around him, Resi also noticed he was the only passenger now on the tram.

"We've passed Leidse plein, haven't we?"

The driver had nodded.

"I thought you were going to tell me when we reached it?" Resi said, standing up and lurching forward.

The driver was suddenly angry. "I told you not to sit behind me, didn't I? I couldn't see you…"

Resi became propitiatory, realizing he was only worsening the situation. He decided the driver was enjoying another lost passenger and even suspected the driver had intentionally overlooked announcing the stop. With great deference Resi asked him what could be done?

"You must get off at the next stop. Then take the tram going back to Auschwitz."

Resi was stunned by this reply. Was it a bad joke on the driver's part, or had Resi simply misunderstood? Something in him almost wanted to humor the reply, for the driver's dislike for his passenger was palpable. Resi came from no ghetto and had never been in one. The driver only wanted to dump him where he didn't belong, and not at some fine building where he'd enjoy the delights of Dutch life, partaking of all the good food and wine the people of Holland had once been deprived of because of fools like himself.

Finally, after an unnecessarily protracted journey, the tram stopped. There was a silence even a deaf person could hear. Years later it was the same strange journey. Nothing would stop Resi from his appointment with the shadow of a woman he sought as if a spirit hiding in the body of another, his own.

In a flash the small, pale boy, with the red shock of hair had danced by him as Resi was leaving the Hotel Nieuw. The rain had abated. Outside on the street he was debating what to do, the pistol inside his coat caused his side to ache with an animistic force. If he would have looked up that moment, at the Nieuw's upper windows, the figure of Sam Jeffrins watching him would have been clearly discernible.

*You follow that boy, or you don't go anywhere,* Resi told himself. A few streets north he guessed where the boy was heading for, a youth hangout called the Hyperion. Laira McKinney once seemed to live in that countercultural palace of music and drug pleasures, dancing many nights away within the multi-tiered recesses resembling Piranesi's drawings of decayed Roman torture chambers. Laira had become, in fact, something of a legend at the place, thanks to her unparalleled free form dancing, barefoot as any Isadora. She was wired from the lacerating meth tripping out her interior, laughing at the sheer outrageousness of life when it never foundered on hedonistic ends.

Resi doubted he'd find the boy there if he got lost in the crowd of revelers, but Resi was good at doubting. In the dark ages he would doubt the dungeon's use; in the digital present he would doubt anyone ascending to heaven in the cyber-cathedrals. For that's what the Hyperion resembled, a wired old church building for online worshippers of the dark arts.

It was indeed a sanctified nightclub for the rebellious young. Its mammoth interior was surreally lit up by lights of every color flashing in electronic abandon, all part of some hallucinating DJ wizard's phantasmagoric invention. To Resi, its smoky air was charged with malevolent joy. Everywhere young punks sported bizarre attire and were emboldened by the pursuit of easy pleasure. He strained to keep the small boy in sight; somehow he was let in without any problem, as if belonging to one of its patrons somewhere waiting for him. Pushing through a torque of bodies Resi soon lost track of him; the boy had simply disap-peared. Several yards behind the welter of bodies separating them, Sam Jeffrins was also in dogged pursuit of Resi, and busily shouted into his phone while pushing people rudely aside until, with a curse, he no longer saw him.

"Resi, you can never disappear in a place like this," a voice behind him said, "and you can never find yourself either."

He stared back at a tall figure dressed in rather elegantly trendy apparel, considering the place. He sensed he was looking at another of Jeffrins' transvestite paramours, yet he couldn't be sure. He wasn't sure of anything at this point. Resi's black gloved hand tightened over the firearm in his pocket.

"I'm going to do you a favor," the regally tall figure said. "I know all about you – or enough, don't you think? Let me offer you rest from your ghost quest! You've been a most benighted wanderer, my friend."

"I suppose you work for Jeffrins like the other drag queen mutants?" was the unvoiced question in Resi's thought balloon.

Drink in hand, she guided him to a nearby alcove (one of many, nestled nook and cranny fashion within the oddly designed club's interior) where they sat at a small table affording an excellent view of the proceedings; although there was still a degree of privacy within the cave-like wooden recess.

"I'll introduce myself. I'm Anne, your liaison for the hour. I'm the poor every-woman's princess! Now you had better settle down a tad, baby. I could have strong-armed mutes crawling over you in a minute."

Resi didn't doubt it. It was amazing how well known he was becoming.

"Do you want a drink?"

"No thanks. I'm on business."

They both lit cigarettes and Resi confided above the din that he wondered if Sam Jeffrins owned the Hyperion along with his other holdings.

"No, but he knows the people that do. And when the word's out on somebody it gets around, does it not?" She sipped her drink with a feline fussiness. "My friends call me Dutchess, by the way, all ten of them."

"We have a lot in common, Dutchess, by trying to find out what's happening. At least we get paid for it."

"Yes, that's it, I'm afraid. Everybody's too damn nosey, I guess. You're hanging around, and people that do usually cross the line."

"In your clumsy way, I suppose you're telling me I shouldn't be here."

"Now that's it exactly, Carlton," Dutchess said, batting her long-lashed eyes that were pools of mascara. "You've become a liability to yourself. And moreover, no one in these quaint haunts wants to deal with you. You represent a great phobia, really."

Resi laughed. "I knew I'd find my shrink sooner or later. In a town full of folks like you..."

The amusement faded somewhat from Dutchess' haughty features, delicately dark as any freshly painted bark. "You know, Carlton," she continued with her false intimacy, chiding him, "You're like a child who will resort to breaking the toys of the adult world, aren't you? You're that marvelously malformed primitive boy, one who can never mature. That's your immediate problem. We cannot have the little boy niggers of the world trashing our ways at all. We will not allow them a proper leeway until they understand their quandary here and provide what must be provided. We make the laws..."

"You're the person of color calling me a boy nigger, Dutchess."

"Aren't you acting like one? Just come clean and face the facts. You're not getting anywhere looking for people, dead or alive, especially little boys or girls, Mr. Para Eye. You're tightening your own noose and we'll do it for you too if you're unable to help us."

Resi shut his eyes and shook his head again, the picture of weariness. "You've lost me. I'm going to make this as simple for you and the merry mutants as I can. I know Sam Jeffrins killed a woman named Laira McKinney, whom you're probably familiar with, some months ago at the Hotel Nieuw. I know where her spirit has been – I just need to find out where her body is. Sooner or later the authorities are going to become aware of the fact she's more than a missing person, understand? Sure, I know the police have questioned you all by now and are reluctant to see your, Sambo pimp, as a prime suspect, at least for now. So help me out, are you sure you have all the case file details?"

"I've tried to offer you compassion and a way out, Resi. You're like a little spy here in Amsterdam! You know how spies are treated once they're caught in the act. In time you'll be seen as the culpable one." She sighed, studying him, tapping her glass with a long blue fingernail. The background rock music approached its loudspeaker crescendo as revelers continued to dance by them, all immersed in the flow of indulgent transcendence.

Resi reached out and overturned the ebony queen's drink. Its contents seeped quickly into the table top's wood grain, some of it spilling into her lap. He wanted to despoil her fashionably trashy look, rip off the tin can lids of her earrings and smear the lurid gunk on her face into a doo-doo pool.

"Oh, Resi," she said, frowning, finding her phone. "They'll hurt you now."

In the moment's adrenalin rush he believed her and overturned the table. Propelled into the vicinity's dark confusion was a spiky shoe tip cutting its way into Resi's forehead as he fell beneath plashing passing boots or bare-feet. He shouted but all noise was submerged by the rave's intensity. He was borne aloft now by a crowd's angry hands, obeying the screaming Dutchess, who announced this was the dance of death. Resi's dismay brought his hand to the gun he revealed for the male attackers, waving it like a cross before the depraved eyes of vampires.

The sound of a gunshot added a fitting counterpoint to the explosive music. Aimed just above a burly bouncer's head, the discharged round freeze-framed the scene as it gouged out a nickel-sized hole in the wall behind him. Forgotten temporarily in the ensuing panic allowed Resi to karate chop his way through any further obstruction and soon he made his way to the nearest exit door.

*Now what?* Resi asked aloud, trapped within another mirrored alcove, one of many secreted in the building's maw of skeletal closets. Trying to right himself, pistol still in trembling hand, he realized the ample liquid he at first thought was sweat dripping down his face was in fact blood. He lunged forward, pounding his way along the wooden wall with the butt of his Beretta, leaving dents as he did so, until he found another door to unhinge and plod through.

It led to yet another alcove. One more dead end.

Resi felt imprisoned within this incredible yet dingy maze of back rooms leading to nowhere. The more he uncovered them, the more his terror accelerated and gave rise to a vibrating screaming he could not control. His body ached afresh from the ballroom mauling and a turned left ankle caused him to limp along now like a pitiful leper escaping the stoning multitude.

At hallway's end, the final room he stumbled into revealed a disturbing pair of mutant transvestites making love atop some antiquated gibbet. Though startled they believed him a surprise addition to their activity and paused to allow Resi to proceed with whatever his panting, gun-wielding theatrics had in store for them. Almost as quickly as he'd entered, Resi was gone, leaving behind the lovers with their crestfallen demeanors and gasps of keen disappointment.

# Chapter 9

# Tracking Fate to the Magister's Conclave

It was all just a temporary diversion that could have lasted an hour or an eternity to Resi. He was a man who had been swept back into some dangerously temporal riptide, yet still was unaware of its ultimate consequences.

Back on the road driving again, all he knew was that he needed serious weapons now, not just to free Laira but himself. The city's teeming populace crisscrossed bridges above brackish tributaries adorned by colorful house boats. Resi's crucial need to reconnect with Laira again had something of a junkie's need about it. People were in cafes or eating fish at outdoor stalls, all beneath the canopy of clouds overhead. They had no idea of an encroaching otherworldly vengeance which would at any moment disrupt their lives with its cataclysmic force.

But he had to get some guns, feeling Jeffrins was somewhere on his trail, and Resi had phone calls to make.

Now sitting in his hydra-electric vehicle as the sky unleashed its torrential rain, Carlton Resi had to admit he was making shaky progress – but at least it was progress. He'd managed to make his escape from the Hyperion after all, with Jeffrins or any of his gang nowhere in sight at the moment.

Earlier, Resi had slithered through the crowd while heading for his car, parked nearby the Hyperion. One person he nearly knocked flat was the Hotel Nieuw's night desk clerk, of all people and Resi knew fate and serendipity knocked on his door. Thanks to a wad of Euros, the young clerk caved in and told him choice secrets about the elusive red-haired little boy. Resi couldn't believe his luck, which continued when he finally was able to reach his Los Angeles office gofer, and Gal Friday extraordinaire, on his replacement phone.

"Where are you?" Ms. Sylph shouted in introduction. "Are you okay, Carlton?"

"In a manner of speaking, I guess so, but let's keep manners out of this."

"Glad to hear it, boss, especially from the horse's mouth... Anyway, hey, I did what you wanted. Your stolen Cypress cell was totally deactivated with memory wiped clean, thanks to Robby, your new tech wiz, who also says hello. He's sitting here eating a pizza with me at the office. Been another long day..."

"Good, go on."

"Also, I emailed you all the background info you wanted on those individuals, namely the Maze Niner research and conservancy institute, Doctor Hiram de Hazeraux, and Rooksana Zu."

Resi had his computer on now, marveling at its colossal memory and tech-spec superiority, before Sylph could take another long-distance bite.

"You do know that Rooksana Zu is a well known investigative reporter for a large Dutch newspaper, don't you, with undeniable political connections? She's also something of an amateur witch with membership in a large international group of similar practitioners."

Resi coughed over his cigarette smoke, opening his car window to let some air in. An investigative reporter and amateur witch...? Well, that was better than her being a female assassin or James Bond girl, he had to admit.

"You've got the complete document files there on everything," Sylph concluded over a prolonged, very audible munch.

"Thanks, I owe you dinner for this one."

"You got it, no problem."

Driving his way to the Magister's controversial conclave, however, proved more and more of a problem as his GPS went on the blink and the directions he'd been given proved sketchy. The conclave was reputedly a short distance from the Magister's residence, but was still proving a bitch to find. Was it nearby the

Artis Zoo, of all places?

Resi decided to call Rooksana pronto, before they would rendezvous together and pursue the very much in demand Hiram de Hazeraux. Over a squealing tire Zu's voice sounded like an exotic alarum, chilling his ear momentarily. Resi continued driving in pell-mell fashion through some wet and tricky cobblestone city streets.

"First off, the shop blood we found is human all right," Zu's voice crackled. "My lab tech doesn't yet know whose it is, however, but I don't think it's Hiram's. The tablet also has him mystified, I had to stop him from doing anything but x-raying it digitally."

"You're better off not touching it," Resi warned, nearly knocking down a matronly bicyclist in front of a pickled herring street stand. "We don't know anything about that, it could be toxic."

"Well, it's been user friendly. You won't believe this – I can't tell if it's predestined or what – but there's a map with detailed instructions on how to get to de Hazeraux's hiding place at Maze Niner, and there are security access codes. Presently it's closed to the public and has high-level security all around it."

"That's good," agreed Resi, "We're either lucky or otherwise – but that won't stop Jeffrins from trying to access the place on his own terms."

"Think we're walking into a trap?"

"We have the tablet that may be a command model he either wants himself, or to manipulate us with it for his own ends, whatever they are…I don't know. But we have to find what he's done with Laira's spirit, or her flesh remains, before Jeffrins does."

"It's like that's the good doctor's trump card, and Laira's energy has directed us there all along, Resi. She's been like his prisoner now, in whatever scientific fashion, just like she was once Jeffrins' sex slave."

"The tablet has to be the potential answer to all of this somehow. But don't touch it anymore, okay?"

"I won't, Resi, I won't. Just tell me when you get those firearms, and where the Magister's conclave is."

"I'd like to know that myself, Zu."

Resi filled her in about his recent fracas and all he'd been up to, along with the revelation that the little red-haired boy was unquestionably just a surrogate son to Laira. "He was like her little gofer, I guess, a whore's bastard who apparently lives on Canal Street. I'd sure like to question the little guy – he may have been with Laira the day she died."

"Put that on your to-do shortlist when we get back," Zu advised him.

He'd be asking Rooksana Zu a lot of questions as well, Resi knew, whenever they returned from de Hazeraux's hangout, if they ever made it that far.

The Magister needed to be filled in as well, and would be in a testily questioning mode whenever Resi arrived for the firearms. The night before in his elegant study was a time for reflection on the jumble of all the recent happenings, and most of all on the personage of Hiram de Hazeraux, the Magister's strange business partner.

The Magister began to question himself more than ever. How many times had he turned on his own SPLANX, as he did now, laying his palm atop the scintillating gray surface – tough and resilient as any diamond texture – until the device registered and identified him (along with every bio-fact of his being, from the physical stats to even the mental ones), hoping to feel the dynamic vibrato course through him with all the powers of the universe that Hiram de Hazeraux had promised? Once again with closed eyes and fluttering eyelids he held his breath in anticipation of the great event finally happening. But, like all the previous times, nothing really happened beyond a series of indecipherable codes and numbers flashing endlessly across the screen, revealing everything and nothing. Once again the Magister brought a liver-spotted fist crashing down in frustration on his desk, so that at least he felt the undeniable fact of pain if nothing else.

He knew de Hazeraux was fixated on the great Italian scientist, Leonardo da Vinci, perhaps to an unhealthy extent. Over a decanter of brandy the Magister dwelled on the implications of such a fixation. During Leonardo's time the human body was venerated and its workings seen as an analogy for the facts of the universe. How far they were from that in the late 21st century, the Magister marveled, adjusting his ornate robe. Now robots were analogies for the operation of the universe and Leonardo's Vitruvian Man was an obsolete being, crucified long ago by pagan worshippers of science. There seemed to be a cruel irony in it all. Leonardo had painted magnificent vistas (if in backgrounds mostly) of nature's strange beauty and inexorable forces that human beings reflected as part of a divine nature, a nature overwhelming all the natural flora and fauna inhabiting the earth. Today mankind was bereft of that divine nature and was more and more endangered by the terrestrial elements he could no longer control. Having been diminished in such a fashion, Man had become a freak, something Doctor Hiram de Hazeraux no doubt found unacceptable.

The invention of the SPLANX tablet, in theory at least, was a technological triumph. Every man would have his SPLANX, and men would improve drastically if the tablet did what it was supposed to do. A new, Ultra-Man would evolve as a result, one who could see through natural creation to the soul of cosmic being itself – and be healthier for it, reborn in a fashion, far from the freakish homosapiens of the present. Let there be a rebirth of the homomorphism of men into harmony with the flowers of good and evil again. This was their mutual goal, the Magister believed, and he'd given a great deal of money to Doctor de

Hazeraux's Neo Eco-Conservancy in the hope of seeing it realized.

Now he had grave doubts all that would happen. Contemporary man was simply an ape, little better than the alien species he had vanquished long ago. The ruins of the Alien War were like the classical ruins of antiquity to the Magister and much of his beloved Holland's natural assets had been permanently damaged. Now, not even a miraculous cyber-tablet costing a thousand Euros could make the long lost flowers grow over the weeds again.

The next day – in the afternoon, Resi was scheduled to pick up the contraband firearms – the Magister did not feel up to par and knew he'd be unable to leave his canal home and venture to the conclave. Instead, an hour or so before Resi was scheduled to arrive, the Magister phoned him, demanding an urgent update on the situation. He had been put off too long, and – reaching for his gold-plated cane – the pain in his legs was no match for the deep chagrin he suddenly felt pressing the phone to his ear.

"I was going to tell you in person," Resi allowed, driving by the Ousterdak. "But I'm glad you called, sir – I may need further directions"

Resi decided then to give the Magister the full facts and recounted in detail what had happened on Spuii when he and Rooksana Zu had entered the SPLANX shop that night and found de Hazeraux's tablet before encountering the Tomu phantoms. He knew the Magister up to now felt out of the loop, but would be immediately awestruck by this confidential news – as indeed he was.

"And you waited this long to tell me, Resi?" the Magister barked in response.

"You wouldn't believe what's happened up to this point, sir, and I've practically lost track of time since we last spoke."

"That was over a full calendar day ago, Resi!"

"Everything's happened so fast, Magister, please do forgive me. My associate, Ms. Zu was injured during an encounter with, well, what appeared to be Tomu creatures. They were horrific ghosts, growing before our very eyes, while exuding a dangerous vibrating energy – or *anti-energy,* really – once the tablet was touched. I was able to circumvent them nonetheless, thanks to the SPLANX tablet, which apparently has critical command capabilities that de Hazeraux controls his experiments with, and God knows what else. And – believe me – the manifested creatures we encountered are within the sphere of his bold and radical inventions and experiments. We're only wondering if he can control the thousands of SPLANX tablets you say have been manufactured for sale – if he'll be able, that is, via the command model we have now, to actually control anyone who might buy these tablets…"

"My sweet God," the Magister uttered, though Resi could barely detect his voice above the traffic and storm sounds.

"There can't be many of those command tablets in existence, Magister. Either your partner wanted someone to find it, or maybe we simply did by chance and his negligence."

The Magister coughed violently and then emitted a string of obscenities Resi easily understood.

"Listen to me, Resi. You're only a minute from the conclave. Do you have that tablet in your possession now?"

"No, my associate Ms. Zu has it."

"Fine… Once you arrive and my man Ebos gives you the firearms, please remain where you are. You're immediately to call Ms. Zu from there and request she bring the tablet to the conclave, do you understand? You will not be able to leave until it is delivered into my possession."

This wasn't what Resi wanted to hear and at first he said nothing for several seconds, realizing his mistake. He then tried to reason with the Magister, saying that retaining the tablet would be crucial to their achieving success or failure at Maze

Niner – along with finding out the true facts of what happened to Laira McKinney.

"I don't care about any of that. I need and want you to get me that tablet. Then I'll advise you on your next course of action, Mr. Resi. In fact our association might be drawing to a close soon, depending on how this pans out."

*My sweet God indeed,* Resi muttered to himself. The Magister had just decided to be a game-breaker. Resi was not sure what de Hazeraux would do once he learned the Magister had the tablet. Would it then become a game-over situation in Maze Niner, and everything pertinent to Laira McKinney suddenly fragmenting into a toxic smokescreen?

"You must bring me that tablet, Resi, or Mr. Ebos will deal with you."

"Please listen, Magister. We have no way of knowing whether or not de Hazeraux can control the tablet we have. It could very well blow up in your face once you have it."

"Bring me the tablet, Resi, and follow my instructions to the letter. Call your associate immediately once you arrive at the conclave! The entranceway leads to our garage and shop facilities, where you'll see Mr. Ebos waiting for you."

The Magister clicked off, leaving only the momentary afterimage of a Rembrandt self-portrait subbing for his own. Resi sighed, cursing his fate. He knew without a doubt Zu would never surrender that tablet. Obviously she knew both de Hazeraux and the late Laira McKinney, possibly due to journalistic articles or interviews and certainly wasn't telling Resi all she knew. Besides, she was working for the two Dawson sisters and certainly not the Magister. Having found the conclave driveway and steered the Peugeot slowly towards its entrance, Resi realized he was between a hard rock and a harder place.

With a sigh Resi braked the car and looked into the visor's cosmetic mirror. Although just pimple-sized on his right cheek (and sometimes a bitch to find), quickly Resi flicked on his somatic GPS-V micro-cam to enable Zu to know, and see, his exact location. What he saw with his own brown eyes failed to thrill him.

He slowly motored through a huge garage-like repair facility as noisy as it was intermittently smoky. Waving to him from a nearby scaffold was the stout figure Resi recognized as Velmer Ebos, the Magister's right hand man, in all things of the lowest common denominator. All about his vehicle, Resi could see a bevy of antiquated motor bikes being rebuilt into more contemporary designs. Resi recognized one such classic, the Porsche Custom Neo-Chopper motorcycle, which had survived remarkably though the decades. One of his favorites, he'd had one in his college days to buzz around on. He knew these were probably black market Choppers that would not be for use anywhere in Holland, but likely for sale to avaricious buyers in other European and international localities.

Resi felt the heat on his cheek expand like a fibrillating pulse and hoped the garage images were streaming into Zu's computer. Hurriedly he stuffed his own into a backpack with his phone and other important equipment, noting a sudden unmistakable pain growing in his right forearm as he did so.

"I have two semi-automatic pistols and ammunition for you," Velmer Ebos said after climbing down from a set of glistening metallic spiral steps. "They're old ones, unfortunately, though refashioned."

"Thank you," Resi replied, quickly examining their handling ease and other technical aspects before putting them into his backpack.

"And I also have this, a real beauty. It's a vintage Zyler-9 Laser Shock, hard to find and experimentally elite to say the least. It fires sonic shock waves capable of beheading a man at fifty yards."

"Wow," Resi muttered, almost petting the weapon. The Shock resembled firearms from sci-fi films and lurid comic books.

"Does the manual come with it, Ebos?" The bluish-black Shock mimicked in design a small machine gun with a pistol grip and came with a shoulder sling that Resi immediately made use of.

Ebos laughed hoarsely, wiping his thick grease-stained fingers with a red cloth. "If you can fire a 9 millimeter pistol from days of yore, you can fire this, comrade…Oh by the way: I've been informed by the Magister you're to wait here until he makes his appearance. He's indeed frail these days and uses a cane, so the interval could be several minutes."

"I see. Well, not a problem."

"He mentioned something about an electronic tablet he wants you to give him. Do you know what he's talking about?"

"A tablet…?"

Resi looked furtively around the repair shop. It was the size of an airplane hangar. Hell, he told himself, an aircraft might suit his needs at present. The diamond diode in his cheek burned like the devil while charting its universe of diametric visions.

"Can you give me the tablet, Resi, and I'll call to save the Magister a trip."

Ebos had motioned to a couple of husky men attired in overalls who now moved decisively towards Resi's car. The paranormal investigator would have sworn he had seen them before at Sam Jeffrins' place. Meanwhile the pattering rain made its arrhythmic presence known outside in the street. As noted in so many areas, an instant in time can equal a moment of eternity. Resi's gamble here was an ongoing sequential process, he knew. Before Ebos could turn his head back from watching his men search the car, Resi had booted the kickstand of an idling Porsche Chopper while knocking down the grease monkey tuning it. In that eternal instant of active motion, Resi mounted the motor-cycle and was gone, whooshing out of the hangar atop a mobile jet taking him back into the convoluted roadways of the town and city.

A worker near the mammoth trash compactor was so startled

by Resi's exit he fell ungraciously beneath the compactor's platen. His head was squashed in an instant.

The screaming of Velmer Ebos could be heard all the way to The Hague.

In her own customized mega-engine, Rooksana Zu had seen it all and was now tracing Resi's path on her computer, while trying to determine his approximate location. Racing her vehicle and somehow avoiding police surveillance monitors by using ultra-block reverse sensors, Zu was making good progress leaving the city behind her.

In open-mouthed surprise she had viewed Resi's bike flight through the rainy environs, hoping he wouldn't spin out. He'd nearly collided with a dozen unwary bicyclists, his Porsche fumes liberally dusting them in passing. His Chopper tires ripped up foxgloves once securely planted in street side flowerbeds, and fallen herb boxes lay in Resi's rumbling wake. On he sped, evading at one point a police car at a busy Amsterdam intersection, before churning towards the Waterland area and outlying districts like the Amsterdam Bos and Lange Bretten, long considered almost wilderness.

Where was he going? After almost an hour Zu realized he was somewhere in Gronigen, a place some 200 kilometers from Amsterdam, at the apex of Holland. The frenetic scenes of his motorcycle escape eventually became a hardly varying image of quasi-countryside, which showed his bike at a standstill now. Only portions of his hands and feet were visible throughout the mad flight, she could see one of his wrist tattoos, confirming what she needed to know, that he was probably all right, yes, and not hurt. Or so she hoped.

In this city of once urban renewal, littered by an overgrowth of untamed plants and weeds, she found him on a quiet and nearly deserted bike path that his somatic GPS-V directed her to.

"What took you so long, Zu?"

She answered his question with her own: "And what, may I ask, happened?"

"Never mind…The Magister dearly wants our tablet. He doesn't want to see it given over to his errant pal, Doctor de Hazeraux, without question," Resi said between gulps from a water bottle she'd given him. Without further elaboration he handed her the revamped pistols from his backpack. "Here, you take these. I've got this heavy Shock bastard that can supposedly knock down bridges with its sonic shock waves…Once I learn to use it, of course."

"Did they follow you?"

"For a while perhaps, yes and no…We have to make tracks for Maze Niner pronto. I learned one thing, something's in my bloodstream allowing Sam Jeffrins to keep track of me. I drank something he gave me that night in town at his place, I'm sure of it. He can determine where I'm at by using a thermal digital monitor traversing great distances. Right now he can determine our coordinates. He's letting me take him exactly to wherever we might find de Hazeraux's hangout."

"What'll we do?"

"I don't want his goons reaching us." Resi pointed to a spot on his right forearm. "It's settled in here, the tracer, I know it. My adrenalin helped me pick it up during the ride. I repeatedly felt it…it's like a pricking sensation, much more painful than simple GPS implants." Resi walked over to the Porsche Chopper where his backpack now was. He took out a small medical case containing a syringe and surgical instruments. "You have to cut it out of me, Zu. It shouldn't be that difficult. Shoot me up with this pain killer, and then drain me."

Rooksana Zu took a deep breath and looked around her. City sounds seeped in like prominent reminders that total privacy was always a thing of the past.

"Do it before someone comes," Resi said, wiping his arm with an alcohol patch.

Zu knew there was little time to debate the issue. She had to be careful, and hopefully pinpoint exactly where the invasive fluid sac was before cutting into Carlton's arm. With his guidance this was somehow achieved and a purple, glistening fluid, slowly emerged along with Resi's blood once she cut him. Resi cried out despite himself and sobbed from the pain as Rooksana swabbed every purple trace from the incision, then wrapped his forearm with surgical bandages.

As he grimaced she held up a small sac-like container her knife had lacerated.

"This was it."

Resi nodded, looking back at her with his serious gaze, slowly saying in a low voice, "You know, all along we've thought dear Hiram wanted us to discover that tablet, to keep Jeffrins from getting it."

"And...?"

"I think it's actually been otherwise, Zu. I think it's been Laira McKinney and her spiritual energy all along. She's responsible for our finding it – she led us to it in a way, just as surely as the Magister or the Dawson sisters. Those Tomu ghosts we triggered by taking Hiram's SPLANX probably weren't spontaneous. And Laira's now part of them, a part of the Tomu." Smoking a crumpled cigarette and wiping sweat from his brow, Resi managed to point a finger towards the sky. "Up in that galaxy, you know? Alive and dead she's helped them in their attempt to come back to earth and reseed it with their fungal and genetically engineered plants, to see if they could grow here what once grew on their own earth. And to see if their life forms could cohabit and evolve with parts of our own. Laira McKinney at first aided their cause while Hiram de Hazeraux performed all kinds of experiments on their behalf, and at their bidding. Laira's been like a queen to them! They're now so close, in a weirdly incestuous way, but I think Laira's now the wild card and wants to stop them. See what I mean? She's turned on them, probably has seen what it will do to us and this planet after all...and now she wants us to help her halt all of them – de Hazeraux, the race of Tomu, Jeffrins, the Magister – all of them..."

"Oh, wow," said Rooksana Zu, in one barely audible whisper.

"And you? What about you, Rooksana? You have to tell me now just what's what between you and her. Between you and everybody of interest...I know you're a journalist of some kind, but I don't think you joined up just for the story."

"I'm her step-sister," Zu finally said, in hardly any confessional way. "We're blood-related, her mother was my mother...But I've never known who my biological father was."

"You're hoping to find that out? Why did you keep this from me for so long?"

"Because it doesn't matter! And you would have become too curious and maybe too demanding, okay? Actually, as a journalist, I'm protecting my vital sources – probably you might want to know them. And that information I can't give you, Resi. Not now or ever. Maybe you have to get that yourself."

Resi took a last long drag off his cigarette and tossed the butt in the direction of the discarded sac residue. "Right, so you're going to play the journalist to the end, is that it? I think you're here for more reasons than finding Laira or what happened to her."

"That would be none of your business."

"Really! *Real*-ly, I don't completely buy that. So tell me something. What's all this business about your being a witch?"

"It's basically unfounded. I'm just an old-fashioned one, of the Wicca variety. Though Laira, my mother and I have always had an interest in the occult."

"And your grandmother, or whomever, had something to do with introducing the Nazis to the Tomu aliens, way back when?"

"Most of that is hearsay. As a family we hated the Nazis, pure and simple. But World War II is, well, an ancient war."

"But it sure had an effect on Holland and the Jews here."

"Maybe so…"

"I would hate to think our Doctor de Hazeraux is carrying on the work of infamous Nazi doctors, wouldn't you?"

"Yes."

"Because the Holland branch of your family is basically Jewish, isn't it?"

"What of it. I'll write about it all for you someday, Resi, and let the true facts fall where they may. But right now we have to get out of here…"

# Chapter 10

# Somewhere in the Maze at Midnight

"They found it," Hiram de Hazeraux said to her in his flawless English, his overly pale face accentuating dirt specks still clinging to it. The Maze Niner lab manager, Alandra Steen, continued to run a damp cloth across the stubble regions of his cheeks. Her own face was a mask of worried concern.

"For a second there…"

"You thought things happened to me back at the Magister's shops?"

"I couldn't reach you now and then by any means. And your command tablet alarm was sending distressing signals."

He grinned out a grimace, sitting at her lab desk, and, warm coffee mug in sweating hands, tried slowly explaining things as carefully as he could. *Wild or large animals are practically non-existent in the Netherlands,* recalled de Hazeraux from a guidebook description he knew might soon become obsolete.

"Who found it, H.H.?" Alandra spoke, breaking the tense silence.

"We must be very careful now." The tall and angular figure of Hiram de Hazeraux loomed warningly over his shorter accomplice. "I was in that shop for a final check in the morning. I know it's taken me a while to tell you, but there's a time for everything in its place, Steen…I made sure the secondary command tablet was in the wall niche, a safe enough place during emergencies, knowing it was up for grabs for whoever would find it."

"Just as you knew it would possibly be," Alandra Steen replied in a sibilant tone, excited despite her fears. "Fate sometimes intervenes in these matters."

"Yes, it sometimes does, one way or another," de Hazeraux agreed, his large dark eyes lingering on framed pictures of buttercups and purple heather, hanging on their main office walls. They were alone, Alandra's workday was technically over and outside, through the picture windows, the last oak and linden trees swayed persistently from the strong winds.

"But as you saw on the CCTV images I remotely uploaded to you, the Magister's detective has a partner I recognized. She's an investigative reporter the Magister never would have hired, but I've been waiting a long time for her. I guess fate has brought her into the picture. It's undoubtedly the Dawson sisters who've done it, and of course they used to visit here frequently, with Laira, way back when."

"I remember, H.H....I once had to give them an extensive tour of all nine of our plant and fauna facilities, sometime before the shutdown. But at least your Magister's man found it, and her return will be like a homecoming."

Alandra Steen was glad that de Hazeraux looked well enough but the knowledge of materializing the Tomu entities still frightened her. It was too early for that, their research and experiments were advancing remarkably, yes. But it was still too early and Doctor de Hazeraux's revelations shocked her to the core. So much so that she was the one who began sweating profusely from an anxiety of nerves.

"I thought their manifesting spirit entities alone would be enough to scare Jeffrins' thugs if need be, but the energy force is hard to control, as I and the Magister's duo found out. You wouldn't believe how it happened; they simply morphed-up instantly into their projected dimensions. Their ferocity and cries were horrific, beyond any of our test readings and beyond anything from our bio-cam sessions. It was like being under a jet engine, and suddenly two of the Tomu monsters appeared and emanated a wave of volcanic energy that tore the place apart and seriously overwhelmed the attackers. One was practically disemboweled before my eyes! By the time I synchronized the tablet specs properly the thugs had vanished out the back, dragging their wounded with them. Then I put the tablet in its hiding place, never realizing more visitors would appear to deal with the lingering Tomu force, and left."

"My Gott, H.H. – those manifestations saved your life!"

"Very possibly, and for awhile I did control them, I did dematerialize the apparitions successfully enough, or I wouldn't be here telling you this."

Hiram de Hazeraux continued staring through the windows, picturing possible goblins with each passing minute. His command SPLANX tablet was on Alandra's desk now and she regarded it as one would a potential explosive. The Maze Niner complex was uniquely located in a large and sprawling geographic wilderness, long gone to waste through government neglect and the abuse of scavengers and bordered in part, and in strategic ways by Lange Bretten (Amsterdam's so called extant wilderness, half a kilometer wide and ten kilometers long), plus ravaged forest areas remotely adjacent to Amsterdam Bos, once one of Europe's largest city parks, before it became a refuge for mutants. Somewhere in those unlikely latitudes you could find what was left of Maze Niner's grounds, though their accessibility had become more difficult through the years. Some media pundits even dubbed it "There Yet Not There," due to its mysterious lore and layout, with some portions aboveground and others apparently not.

Funded as a private enterprise by an illustrious group of board members, the Maze's original purpose – according to its co-founders – was to initiate ways and means to revitalize Holland's stricken terrain. Scientific research and experimental procedures spearheaded this attempt to salvage endangered Dutch flora and fauna before the aftermath of the Alien War imposed an irrevocable devastation, impossible, perhaps, to alter by the coming century.

Eventually funding disappeared for the Maze Niner institute and its co-founders badly needed a way to find viable finances.

Their last hope for financial salvation was the Magister, of course, whom Hiram de Hazeraux had successfully recruited as a primary business partner for the SPLANX tablet program. If all went according to plan, SPLANX would be the centerpiece of the new Maze Niner promotional well-being program, which included revitalizing human beings – not just flora and fauna. It would pay huge dividends, both for the Magister and the institute, if SPLANX became a money-making blockbuster capable of getting their enterprise from the red to the black – and, more importantly, changing public perception of Maze Niner into being the force for ecological rebirth and reinvigoration, rather than the opposite.

"We may be a forgotten hamlet in the Netherlands boondocks," Doctor Alandra Steen said. "But one day we'll be as important as the Dutch parliament to the people."

At this, Hiram de Hazeraux raised a skeptical eyebrow, for to him the Dutch parliament was obsolete, thus her saying had to be an oxymoronic one. Thinking this over he laughed discreetly, looking out the office windows, listening to the music of the wind. What really mattered was the SPLANX command tablet he had devised in secret for his own use – something the Magister had known nothing about at one point – the very tool necessary for reconverting Tomu fungal DNA from the distant past into resuscitated states of existence extraordinary, to say the least, and a powerful force combining dead matter with living spirit to set governments on their heels.

Now this tablet was in the hands of the Magister's investigators and there was nothing de Hazeraux could do but wait. Fate had deemed it so.

There was more to his dilemma, of course. Sam Jeffrins and his terrorist operatives wanted in on the action and would turn the tablet deals for profitably destructive ends. Amazingly Sam Jeffrins found out about it all because of Laira McKinney. The abducted subject Hiram de Hazeraux was able to study and experiment on had ratted on him. And just when H.H. had needed to continue studying her more, Laira McKinney fulfilled her suicidal destiny by encouraging Jeffrins to murder her. With almost bitter irony de Hazeraux recalled how he'd paid the little red-haired boy who followed Laira to bring back parts of her butchered body for further study, hoping to complete his mission.

They had been through so much together, Alandra Steen thought. They had worked together on environmental improvement projects for years. She brought tentatively exploratory fingers to the face de Hazeraux had transplanted onto her after the lab fire accident, fifteen years before, when she had been burned almost beyond recognition.

Alandra still remembered her seared face, seeing it more clearly in memory than ever. Gone were her nose, lips, ears and eyelids, with only a beet red flatness of scars and a twisted mouth remaining. Yet de Hazeraux, along with his facial re-constructors had saved her, somehow they had fashioned a new visage, making it possible for her to work in Maze Niner and go about in public again.

She loved H.H., of course. They made a great team in the salad days of Maze Niner, which was once a flora and fauna fantasyland open to the public. The interest in their most privately funded project was overwhelming at first. The Dutch natives paid money to see how the future of their polder areas, farmsteads and expansive fields would progress with ecological improvements. After all, Amsterdam was once a center for the study of natural history. Nature scientists had once inventoried and classified all the exotic plants and animals brought to the city by maritime explorers.

At Maze Niner newly engineered plants and their hybrid growths were truly groundbreaking and pointed a way to making the city, its dune landscapes, waterways, and Lange

Bretten wilderness revitalized and fully thriving again. Alandra Steen and her controversial partner were almost folk heroes at one point, something they had never intended – and something that led to an increasing critical pressure from assorted dignitaries, in local political and scientific circles, much alarmed at their unorthodox experiments and hybrid creations deemed 'otherworldly.' Such was the word used by certain elements of the media, less than enthusiastic over the promise of Maze Niner to make Holland's flora flourish again.

Once in Amsterdam Bos – or Green City Park – there had been one hundred and fifty indigenous tree species and two hundred or so bird species in an area covering more than one thousand hectares, but the post-Alien War years adversely changed all that. So many plants and animals had been vitiated. Common trees like beech, oak, pine and elm became endangered; the cherished flowers too, buttercups, daisies, and tulips became diseased, and the purple heather of heaths in September turned a sickly brown.

The donated funds for natural conservancy projects quickly hit the skids as well and Doctor Steen began to fear her working and private relationship with Hiram de Hazeraux would soon wither.

At about that time, however, Hiram had told her of his new experiments in his secluded lab behind the Maze Niner complex. Only a few individuals really knew where the bunker actually was, since it was a relic from the Alien War era, overgrown by dense foliage, secluding it from the complex at large and officially off limits at that. But since Doctor Hiram de Hazeraux was the site Director and co-founder of Maze Niner – and a good friend of the Magister, chief patron of the program now – he was able to commandeer the ancient lab for his own research and projects.

Only Alandra Steen really knew of the particulars. Her partner told her he had found toxic fungus specimens leftover from the war, obviously of Tomu origin, which he'd begun experimenting with in several unique ways. Alandra had gratefully assisted him in his private activities, which went beyond what they had achieved for Maze Niner's developmental program.

This was something entirely different and radical, Hiram claimed, something akin to his search for an Alien God Particle, the galactic equivalent of the Higgs Boson within particle physics. Of course to continue his search he needed some form of alien life matter, which his discovery of the toxic fungus left by the slain Tomu invaders fortunately provided him.

Hiram de Hazeraux had become ecstatic again, describing all this over a cup of coffee in their secret house outside Amsterdam, a safe haven, and Alandra thanked her lucky stars. Maze Niner itself might flounder, but their private investigations would only flourish. The tall doctor with his shock of ebony hair assured his partner they would soon make headway, for they were working non-stop devising a digitally enhanced tablet which somehow harnessed the Alien God Particle's energy.

"If only Sweden knew of it, we'd win the Nobel Prize!" Alandra exclaimed.

H.H. would somehow be able to summon energy manifestations of the ghastly Tomu beings, he told her. "But can we control this energy without its turning destructive?" In a sense it was like manifesting ghostly plasma via scientific means – i.e., via the tablet, which Alandra would soon dub, SPLANX, simply because the name came to her.

"We can devise a similar tablet on a lower energy level, giving people a 'burst' of the God Particle to make them feel better. We can sell the idea to the Magister and see if he goes for it," de Hazeraux concluded.

"And in so doing we raise money from him to continue resurrecting Maze Niner, while we keep working on the command tablet for your Tomu experiments as well," said Alandra, raising her porcelain cup of java to toast her partner.

Toasting her as well, Doctor de Hazeraux added, "We've been

working with so-called 'dead' galactic DNA from the Tomu, yet have achieved all this."

"Are any of them still alive on their planet, do you think?" Alandra wondered. Absently with a forefinger she traced the thin circular scar outlining her transplanted face.

"Only their energy is left," de Hazeraux ventured, his morose expression deepening. "I believe they were all killed during the war. Only their fungal mold remnants are left here, lingering like old tree stumps. I must *will* them back to us."

"Then we must facilitate their full-bodied return indeed, Hiram. If that were possible you could scare the world back to its very roots."

"If that were possible, there would be no need for war anymore, would there, Steen?"

Nearby a small android creature scooting about laughed at de Hazeraux's remark. It was a robot-like replica of Stanislaw Lem, a renowned 20th century science fiction author. Hiram regarded it as the lab mascot, capable of fetching him coffee among other light tasks. He asked the lab android what he thought of it all.

"We don't want to conquer the cosmos, we simply want to extend the boundaries of Earth to the frontiers of the cosmos," the little Lem said. "A dream will always triumph over reality, once it is given the chance. It is not good for a man to be too cognizant of his physical and spiritual mechanisms. Complete knowledge reveals limits to human possibilities, and the less a man is by nature limited in his purposes, the less he can tolerate limits…Either something is authentic or it is unauthentic, it is either false or true, make-believe or spontaneous life; yet here we are faced with a prevaricated truth and an authentic fake, hence a thing that is at once the truth and a lie…To torture a man you have to know his pleasures."

"Well spoken, dear Lem," complimented de Hazeraux. "Now give me a back rub, won't you?"

Somewhere in the Maze, nature had devolved into a bizarre replication of its former being, Zu knew. As she wheeled her Porsche super X-2 sedan over battered roads only half-paved, Rooksana wondered if she could keep her vehicle with its mega-engine intact, so horrendous was the terrain her huge tires churned through. Above them the skies were evolving into darkening cloud masses, shot through with awesome lightning bolts. The storm was regenerating itself instead of losing force and form. The charred earth they sometimes had to slow down to muddle through was strewn with strange craggy remnants from the Alien War: black metal slag fragments shaped like amorphous trail markers from past massive devastation alternated with eerie plants, half-dead or otherwise. Zu kept excitedly pointing out all this to Resi as she drove.

It was an amazing landscape of alien plant morphology, Zu decided. Something rife with hybrid growths achieved via, and/or destroyed by, a genetic tampering with both terrestrial and extraterrestrial fungi. She recalled the importance of fungi flowers and plants as decomposers because, coupled with bacteria, they regenerated crucial elements like phosphorous and nitrogen back into the ecosystem. Yet something was wrong here; even in the increasing nocturnal gloom the Porsche headlights revealed an eco-system gone to almost complete decay, something the fires of conflict alone could not bring, since much of what Zu saw had been the failed attempts of soil rejuvenation and extensive replanting of diverse flora.

But what kind of corrupted plants were here? She recognized some that reminded her of Phallus impudicus, a member of the phallus-like stinkhorn family (Phallaceae); incredibly huge and hardly indigenous within this Netherlands area, they nonetheless still smelled foully beneath blue-bellied flies spinning around the numerous spore-laden and viscous bodies standing like an army of slime molds in the night.

"This is incredible," she gasped aloud to Resi, whose eyes

were fixated more on his computer imagery than anything outside.

"This is disgusting, you mean," he replied, blocking his nose with a wrinkled handkerchief. "What *are* those? There better not be too many we can't get around."

There were more of the huge and odoriferous plant horrors indeed and Resi kept remarking how it appeared they were driving through fields of gigantic plant phalluses, illuminated by his maglight.

"Mother Nature has a bizarre sense of humor," Zu agreed, "but men did this." Though having what she considered just a rudimentary knowledge of plant biology, Zu explained to Resi how fungi like these begin as egg-like bodies beneath the earth, until an erect and phallus-stalk knifes into the egg, forming a cupped basal volva for the quickly elongating stalk. Each plant phallus head they saw was slick with darkly mucopurulent spore slime, and each one resembled some misplaced phallus of an unknown force.

The spinning flies were upon them like a mass of locusts and Zu barely got her window up in time. They both shouted from the sudden blast their speeding vehicle was greeted by, and – nearly blinded – Zu couldn't decide whether to slow down or keep speeding through the clouds of malignant flies now splattering endlessly against her windshield, leaving amber trails of glittering, mucous-like remnants there.

In a terrifying instant the Porsche veered off the road and Zu found herself roughly navigating between the totem-like, phallic plants, looming as grim sentinels, blocking her path everywhere. Resi had been forced back into his seat, luckily with his seat belt on, and barely could keep holding his laptop. Definitely this wasn't what he had signed on for. He was a seeker of human ghosts, not ones from space, the irony kept gnawing at him – even as he was jostled about so violently in this joyride that he wanted to curse every living and dead thing because of it.

Then, just as abruptly, the wave of flies parted and the Porsche was back on the bumpy road leading them further uphill, away from the pillar-like phalluses, and into a more recognizable moonlit landscape.

Resi audibly sighed, still hugging his computer and keeping a tight hold on the SPLANX tablet, he uttered oaths loudly. He managed to glance at his watch and saw – unbelievably – that the hours had advanced as minutes might. This Maze Niner territory he had heard about was indeed uncanny.

They kept going, turning down and onto many difficult and secluded roadways, with Resi giving Zu directions according to the SPLANX tablet GPS guidelines he read from. Up to this point they had encountered no one else, either on foot or otherwise, so deeply were they now in an enclave doubtless few had been able to venture into. Its desolate aspects resembled a hazardous mine field, an area whose warning signs and barriers they had disregarded and were able to easily ignore, since to the Dutch government the area surrounding the Maze Niner was simply a wasteland of little value now that the attempts to turn it into a wildlife preserve for neo-flora and fabulous fauna (an amusement park for the senses, really) had failed so miserably through the years. Without the tablet they would be irretrievably lost, Resi knew, and even now he totally felt so.

As they bumped along over the crest of the great hill, and then down it, the dawn's filtering sun glinting gradually dissipated the night's putrid gloom. Now they could see through the ruined forest areas surrounding them, now they could espy evidence of what had recently happened. They passed decimated small buildings and scattered human bodies wearing uniforms with Maze Niner emblems and insignia. A chill went through Zu and Resi as they stopped here and there to examine the bodies amid the wreckage. Rooksana snapped numerous photos of it all on her cell phone camera.

Resi knew what it meant.

"They're up ahead, hiding and waiting for us all right," he said, squinting through a pair of binoculars at the distant terrain a fog seemed to hesitantly envelop.

"Who is?"

"Who do you think – Sam Jeffrins and his mutant thugs...Things are beginning to add up. I know I saw some of them back at the Magister's conclave. They're with him! They have to be."

"You mean Jeffrins and the Magister are partners?"

"Yeah, at the moment it seems so. Maybe one or the other has the real control now. At any rate, they're together, waiting for us to gain access into the Maze — "

"Then they follow, take the tablet from us, and seize control of the Maze complex from Hiramde Hazeraux," Zu said.

"It would definitely fuckin' seem so, Zu."

"What'll we do?" asked Zu, checking her pistols.

"That Zyler-9 weapon I ironically got from the Magister better send out some bad ass shock waves to get us there – and beyond."

Why had Ebos given it to him back at the conclave? Perhaps it wasn't worth a shit and Resi would find out the weapons he had scored and badly needed, were only pacifying peashooters. On the other hand, if Zyler-9 kicked ass, then that meant the Magister and Jeffrins were fighting one another to the very end and he and Zu were game-breakers. No matter what, the Magister's man Ebos didn't want Jeffrins to get that tablet if at all humanly – or *in*humanly – possible.

Ebos had disobeyed the Magister by not stopping Resi and by giving him the weapons to deal with Jeffrins. He would still have a fighting chance against Jeffrins, or whatever else was waiting for them.

"I'll bet you anything that Jeffrins is an underground operative for the Dutch police, or the local corrupt politicians," Resi said, examining the controls of his high-tech, bazooka-like

Zyler-9 weapon.

"Or maybe even the CIA?"

"God, I hope not. That might make him a patriot."

The GPS coordinates took them deeper into a more bush-tangled terrain, smelling of unpleasant mustiness and animal presences. The GPS took them to a seeming dead end, in fact; a cliff-side where all roads ended and desolation remained the key visual component.

Overhead the skies darkened again, heralding an early midnight, and scattered raindrops fell. The rainwater felt hot – too hot, Resi believed. They'd be in literally hot water if its temperature increased. Resi took out his thermal camera, looking for a hot spot in the cliff-side wall, while Rooksana tried chopping away with her knife at some knotty underbrush she hoped was covering a door or entranceway. They were abruptly aware of a gruff, disembodied voice speaking to them in Dutch.

"You won't find a damn thing," the voice said, this time in English. Its owner was nowhere in visible form around them.

Resi began moving his electro-magnetic force detector in the direction the voice came from. They heard nothing more for a while and simply stared in disbelief at one another with their guns raised. Gradually an apparition took shape nearby the cliff wall, something Resi didn't need one of his instruments to detect. It kept taking on the neon-like outline of a large human form, though other details such as its face remained indistinct and ambiguous. Distant widgeons unaccountably quacked out in murky air as Zu and Resi stared incredulously at what was developing before them.

"I have no real name, but am called the Artificer," the dark figure said. "You are not welcome here. No human being is ever welcome for straying into where it doesn't belong."

Resi continued to film the cold presence with his Flir thermal camera, almost as a detached cameraman might.

"We don't mean anything any harm," Zu announced in the shimmering figure's direction. "We respect this place and are trying to reach the Maze Niner underground complex."

"Maze Niner, yes," the figure spoke drone-like, digitally so. "All of this here and its grounds were once the Maze Niner natural preserve. There was once a large lake with a new species of fish life people paid money to see. There was a forested preserve here also, for boars, small mammals, barnacle geese and giant woodpeckers. New plants flourished in the Great Bog with its unique flowering meadows and distinct marsh trefoil, a beautiful hybrid plant with exotically colorful blossoms that many blue throat birds died pecking at."

"I'm so sorry to hear that," Zu said, lowering her gun to her side. "This must have been the most sublime attraction once."

"The black grouse with their red heads also died. They've been extinct for many years," the figure methodically droned on. "The once most common tree, the Scots pine, can no longer grow here. It was fatally corrupted – only its remnants remain."

"Why are you called the Artificer?" asked Resi, disliking having to listen to this Maze tour guide. Nonetheless he behaved as if addressing a spirit presence.

"Because what isn't destroyed is artificial," the shimmering outline spoke. There was no petulance in its voice, only a factual manner.

"We don't understand," Zu said.

"You can't understand. You are still human. And for years your species has destroyed what isn't."

"That sounds like a conundrum to me," Zu insisted. "If you're the artificer, aren't you artificial? Haven't you been made by some intelligent being?"

"You have made me by being conscious of what I'm not. That is why I would destroy you, until you're unconscious of me."

Resi put the thermal camera down. He disliked where this was all going and slowly retrieved his Zyler-9 while Zu kept the figure engaged in conversation. He heard what sounded like angry wild dogs uncontrollably barking nearby. It had been a while since he'd felt such a completely overwhelming disbelief and fear.

"Show us the way into the Maze Niner complex," Resi ordered the shimmering figure. He had his weapon aimed at the Artificer's mid-section.

"The way in is the way you must make."

"Don't talk shit to us now."

Resi had raised his voice so much that Zu looked at him, alarmed.

"I am just a reflection of all that you will never see."

"That's bullshit."

"I am the conscience of all dead things."

"We are not dead yet, and we're still waiting to live."

Resi felt caught in a game he didn't wish to play. The hot pellets of rain had picked up again and were severely pelting him.

"I am the conscience of living things."

"Then you're saying you're both dead and alive, aren't you," Zu accused. Her hands shook as she did so.

"The way in is the way out as well."

"This is the Buddha's apparition, Rooksana," Resi said with a forced laugh. "He's really a video game Buddha, not an Artificer!"

"Show us that," Zu said now, almost angrily positioning her finger on the pistol's trigger.

"You hold the Buddha's heart," droned the figure.

"He means the tablet," Zu said, looking at Resi. Then it dawned on her. The figure itself was the way in. She advised Resi of this as she cautiously moved forward. "Don't!" Resi warned her, but Zu's next action was a leap of faith.

She jumped into the figure's darkness.

# Part III

## The Tomu Cataclysm

# Chapter 11

# A Standoff at the Fountainhead

Rooksana Zu understood she would give herself to SPLANX – yes, she would go that far to see her sister, alive or dead, again. In whatever state de Hazeraux now had her in, Zu wanted to see it, even if that state was powered by the God Particle of SPLANX and posed a threat to her by being exposed to its controversial components. SPLANX was a bio-electronic godhead she surmised, one no doubt connected by a digital umbilical cord to the evolving Tomu creatures, engineered clandestinely by its tablet master.

Zu had to see the results with her own eyes when they drove through the Maze Niner grounds. Her sister, Laira's fate would be partially Rooksana's own, yet she almost welcomed it.

Once inside the lab bunkers, Rooksana questioned her decision as her heartbeat quickened while walking through the dim and fungal-smelling corridor. She reassuringly felt the twin pistols in each pocket of her faux-leather overcoat, shining with a silvery sheen beneath the intermittent ultraviolet light posts. It was cold, unbearably frigid as she warily proceeded through another arm of the maze de Hazeraux had inherited from the Alien War days, which essentially were more nocturnal than otherwise during the purification struggles, and more moss-infested than obstructed by the scattered rocks coated by a lingering algae she found miasmic. Rooksana cursed the tunnel and bemoaned the fact that her phone now failed to work within it. She and Resi were truly left to their own devices.

She paused, almost stumbled rather, through huge and rust-hinged metal doors until the tunnel stopped. It opened onto an extraordinary vista of lab machinery and extensive plant receptacles that throbbed with advanced vegetable life. Blue, skittering liquid infused every plant stem, root, or hybrid fungus plant sequestered in each glass-covered mold towering before her. Inside this underground biosphere was the equivalent of a man-made jungle with artificial illumination, and the energy emanations of the plants nearly overwhelmed her.

More overwhelming was the spectacle of Laira McKinney's form (hybrid-born with elongated, ape-like arms, her face almost a regal mask of something alien yet human) looming gigantically before her. Laira's huge figure wore an opalescent shroud, glittering like incendiary diamonds, and it emanated fire in a pulsing and holographic way from a ruby red fountainhead composed of intricately designed crystals streaming into it. The icy wind it exuded froze Zu to the spot; somehow she felt a desire to raise the SPLANX tablet before it, the way Moses had the stones on which divine commandments were etched. One power would equal another and each would have its opposite force, perhaps creating a greater one.

And *he* was there, waiting for her, of course, watching her all the while in his clinically detached manner.

"Now put your right hand on the tablet's face," de Hazeraux instructed her. With eyes closed Zu did as she was told, feeling a unique vibration invading her fingers...Through her tinted glasses she could see a Byzantine like web of designs form on the tablet's screen, where her fingertips were now glued and whatever force inhabited SPLANX now coursed inexorably through her, until her body imploded wondrously from innumerable sensations pleasurable beyond belief. She felt transformed in an excruciatingly joyful way, the atoms in her body giving way to a dematerializing transition of matter and anti-matter, into a black hole of energy, dark matter itself generated – and for a timeless instant, Zu felt reborn again to something language or conventional constructs of reality had no explanation for.

She was inside a light year, travelling from start to star, galaxy to galaxy, ocean to ocean. She was one with the beginning of all things, seeing humanity as it was born in the crucible of constellations, forged from the breast of Tomu gods, passing by her in infinite splendor, their glowing primate faces the size of great planets, all welded into one anthropoid edifice equaled only by our sun.

This was the miracle of SPLANX, Rooksana knew; this was a feeling and levitation nothing in human terrestrial life could ever come close to and Rooksana Zu wanted never to leave it. It was a merging of both life and death into something known only to the Tomu beings.

It was also somewhere where her sister, Laira McKinney's spirit permanently dwelled, and could never return from.

"You're her sister in the flesh. You have the hybrid DNA accessible for the Tomu cataclysm to come. You must give them the tablet you have, Rooksana, which codes the procedures needed to join their DNA with your own. It has been arranged to happen tonight, when their craft will descend to visit us. You're the descendant, the last one of Lara's clan, and I knew you would come, didn't I? And so did Laira in her eco-transcendent state…a moment she wanted beyond anything else."

*You know that to be true* echoed through Zu's hyper-alert thoughts. It was what Laira indeed wanted, what she had sacrificed herself for.

"The Tomu both abducted and experimented on her," de Hazeraux went on, his bearded features sweating profusely. "They sent her back for me to complete the project."

"You implanted her with the fungal emollient you did research on," Zu replied matter-of-factly. "What came from the alien horticulture thriving in here. Toxic to humanity, a weapon you and any terrorist could use again for your own ends. She was your elite guinea pig."

"I had to. Laira wanted it…She wanted humanity to change

the world. She let a subhuman kill her, however, and spitefully almost ruined everything." Hiram de Hazeraux knew his reasoning had to be absolutely credible to Zu. "She let a fool, Sam Jeffrins, kill all that was inside her that I would have been able to study and monitor in our own subterranean atmospheres."

"I don't believe it," Rooksana said, though she believed otherwise. "You murdered her as much as anyone, with all that you had done to her."

"Did I? Look at the evanescent and eco-plasmic state she has revealed to you. Isn't she beautiful, Rooksana? She's in a place where gods are, and where Jane Dawson always said she wanted to go. To rejoin her heritage, see her mother and grandmother again. She's done that! And she's let you *know* that."

Rooksana fingered the gun beneath her coat. "You're quite a magician with your smoke and mirrors, de Hazeraux, I'll give you that."

The disheveled doctor stopped his pacing, staring now intently at her. "I suppose you'd rather write about this and debunk the amoral Maze Niner scientists, wouldn't you? Meanwhile the world and our country would continue to environmentally deteriorate. Do you think I'm really trying to develop a mass toxin for terrorist use? Bullshit. I'm trying to help your sister's vision come true. I'm trying to make it possible for both the Tomu and humanity to shake hands and form a permanent partnership to make life on this earth habitable for us all, to improve and restore it ecologically from the horrors of war and industrial defoliation...That's what I'm trying to do, Zu, before the likes of Sam Jeffrins take it away from us for their violent ends. Can't you just fucking understand that? We have to learn to live with the Tomu on this planet before their own dies – or our own earth will also."

*Then why did Laira martyr herself,* Zu thought, *to become a goddess?* Or to spur on something that was inevitable since she had gone too far. She had been entrapped by too many things, and – like the perennial lab creature in the maze – reached a cul-de-sac, born to death again and again.

With her pistol now pointed directly at Hiram de Hazeraux, Rooksana Zu quietly asked, "Who made me? Who was my real father, you son of a bitch?"

"You were made from Tomu DNA in a test tube, Rooksana, blended with the Magister's sperm," the doctor replied, just before the warning sirens sounded.

Zu fired point-blank at the doctor's chest, blowing him away.

It was a sterile white corridor leading him on and on, and Carlton Resi kept following it, no matter what. Running through it actually, for his very life, with the Zyler-9 cocked and held high in his right hand. He'd been in many mazes before – hell, wasn't all of life a maze?

It had all occurred in the seeming instant, just as the creation and destruction of worlds was. One second he was at that cliff-side, watching Rooksana disappear into the Artificer's dark figure; the next he was shooting it out with Jeffrin's thugs as they descended from the dark hill towards him.

Thanks to Ebos, he was able to neutralize the situation with the incredible gun in his hands. The imprint of his thumb on its amber button was enough to emit a devastating series of shock waves, disintegrating all the bullets and bodies coming his way. In mid-air a crackling nuclear fission with what once had been metal, flesh, and molecular bone fragmented into microscopic bits of brain matter that floated almost peacefully around him in the detonation's aftermath. Sonic beams with laser capability were no laughing matter; the nuclear gunsmiths had all but perfected such destructive capability.

Was Sam Jeffrins in that floating mush of medulla he wondered? Resi didn't speculate for long. A stray assault weapon's bullet fired by a surviving gunman nearly took off his head. He made a split-second decision to emit a full-blast shock wave in the direction of where Zu had leaped into the Artificer's black hole. Incredibly the hillside diffused into an air of blinding white light, and the very next second he knew he was in the Maze – and running. Running for all he was worth.

All his equipment except the Zyler-9 seemed gone, but he knew Zu had the tablet. The holy grail to all those desperately seeking to possess it...Resi laughed bitterly as this crossed his fervid mind. At the end of the corridor would he find her again, still holding the miracle SPLANX?

In another part of the Maze, at the end of the corridor Resi ran down, Alandra Steen glanced up from the CCTV monitors in the main lab. A look of shock paled the contours of her transplanted and usually bland face. The unthinkable was happening, she immediately buzzed Hiram's intercom – only to get an unremitting static. The thugs were breaking in! The henchmen of Sam Jeffrins, that Hiram warned her about had somehow made it into the hiding place, the underground lab complex that de Hazeraux had once facetiously dubbed 'The Bunker.'

She was so busy with her work she had forgotten all about the minimal security forces posted outside in what had once been the Maze Niner park land, but now was a veritable charred wasteland due to a variety of factors like sabotage from dissident guerrilla political groups or simply a widespread environmental decay. Outside was a burned-out Disneyland of eco-system failure. Inside, the hidden lab complex had thrived for years, and so had its various experiments.

The guards were either dead or captured, Alandra saw, studying the monitors; plus any phone contact to them was dead too. She frenetically picked up her cell phone to directly call de Hazeraux while watching the main interior monitors. They had somehow by passed electronic security codes and were in the corridor leading to her office headquarters. With barely controlled whimpering sounds accompanying her nervous gestures, Doctor Steen tried to lock all the critical office doors via a remote switch – but that failed her as well.

Nothing was working – even most of the computers were down – and sudden shrill sirens warned of an imminent security breach she should have heard minutes before. Where were her aides, Myra and Franz? They had disappeared and were unreachable also, no doubt overwhelmed by the motley and vicious thugs.

She screamed. Windows were being cracked despite their resistant capabilities. Hiram would not, or could not, pick up his cell phone, despite the widespread warning system now in effect. A grim dizziness assaulted her but she told herself to stay strong.

Explosions blew out the doors as Doctor Alandra Steen dived beneath a nearby counter. She was wedged against the wall and choking on smoke when a brute's hand grabbed her, pulling Steen to her feet.

It was Sam Jeffrins. She had seen pictures of him and his mutant followers when Hiram had briefed her some time back. He pulled his trademark watch cap off his now bald head to reveal a bleeding pate crisscrossed by old scars and newer ones. He was indeed a mutant operative of the political state she and Hiram had been fighting for so long.

"Where is he, bitch? Tell me before I rip your false face off —"

She and Hiram had worked on a variety of projects for so long, including the creation of a vast and hybrid underground forest. They had been safe, totally forgotten by the world at large – but not by Sam Jeffrins, the Magister, and Jane Dawson's ex-pat group. Now their sanctuary was violated by a barbarian and Alandra Steen was afraid. While Jeffrins' men and muscled dykes frantically searched her offices, looking for what they probably couldn't understand how to use even if they found it, Steen remained silent to the end. She would simply not cooperate. She fingered the Jewish medallion she wore around her neck, chanting a Hebrew prayer as the intruders attacked her.

Jeffrins' knife was swift, cutting off her face in an instant, revealing the old disfigured one that still looked out in horror at his final thrusts.

"Laira, please...*please* help me..."

Rooksana Zu fell to her knees beneath the crystal fountainhead her sister's ghostly form spouted up from. Vapors swirled like cloudy remnants around her nude and mammoth figure, whose hands and arms gyrated with snake-like sinuosity. "Please! Help me, Laira..." From her backpack Zu produced family mementos as offerings to place before the hissing and vibrating fountainhead with its diverse designs. There were cameo portraits of her mother, father, grandmother and other family members. There was also an old family bible and jeweled crucifix among the offerings. Zu began to weep with begrimed hands covering her stricken face, wanting only to see darkness if darkness indeed was the only truth.

She had all but forgotten the artificial forest around them with its queer mixture of fungal plants and forested tracery of red, pod-laden limbs. Every part of the great sub-terrestrial forest began to tremble with a strange life to its very roots, all somehow the antithesis of any known biology. The pods began to enlarge until they were the size of great boulders, dropping their crimson fruit to the factitious earth. From each pod a plant-like being came forth, only to morph slowly into a hideous apish creature, exuding slime from every orifice and growing wings as it did so. Gradually Rooksana opened her eyes to this unaccountable spectacle as her sister's figure continued to sway with kinetic energy above. In a breathless moment hundreds of the Tomu creatures took flight like a whooshing battalion of bats. Zu fell to the ground as if hit by shearing wind, and the Tomu aliens (born again from some great power, perhaps of her sister's making) spun out and upwards in a crepuscular flock, towards the tunnel of light before her.

All kinds of discordant sounds assaulted Zu's ears, from the forest's whine with the escaping Tomu creatures and the harsh whipping of their newly formed wings, to the emergency sirens ceaselessly blaring everywhere. Zu, grunting, crawled past de Hazeraux's inert body and noticed his own SPLANX tablet lit up like a Christmas bulb on the ground. Without hesitating she placed it in her swollen backpack. Now she had the only command set of SPLANX tablets extant, they reposed like salt and pepper shakers in her possession, each one technically the perfect complement to the other. ("Male god, female god," she recalled de Hazeraux telling her. "The name Mona Lisa is derived from AMON L'ISA…The two tablets together consolidate the opposite forces in the universe to create the ultimate divine One.")

Zu was determined to exit this insane forest, back into the real earth outside, where she would wait for the alien visitation.

Back in the tunnel, Resi, realized he wasn't just running through an underground corridor. It was part of some scientific atom-smashing accelerator which – much later, when reason returned to the earth, along with his brain – he knew could only be part of Hiram de Hazeraux's research. Feeling much like a sub-atomic particle himself, was he the equivalent of the still elusive Higgs Boson, or God particle, awaiting the proton beams that would collide with his body, halving the space between reality and unreality, life and death, being and non-being?

Carlton Resi didn't have time to debate the issue, for unreal flying, ape monsters were winging his way at super speeds. Perfect for sighting-up with his Zyler-9 shockwave dispenser, and that's exactly what he did. In essence he carved his own path through the center of the oncoming Tomu flock, parting that sea of wild wings like a bearded prophet did the Red Sea.

Then he was there, at the edge of the rainbow-hued fountainhead where the vision of a mesmerizing and fantastic figure of Laira McKinney's space-spirit fulminated above him. *Smash these protons*, Resi thought, mentally addressing the colossal spirit still whirling in endless motion. It had to be illusory, yet if he'd had his ghost-detecting equipment he surely would have investigated it. Wind from the spirit's Shiva-like, dancing form, all but bowled Resi over, nearly causing him to lose hold of the Zyler-9. There was no sign of Zu and Resi's heart dropped.

Then bullets whizzed their way past him and Resi knew Jeffrins was in the house. He feared Zu was Sam's prisoner, or even worse. To his right about six of Jeffrins' bone-crushers came from nowhere and, thanks to a powerful bolt from the Zyler, were quickly parted from their molecular make-up.

"The tablet, Wop, just hand over the fucking tablet!" Jeffrins shouted from somewhere behind the fountainhead.

"I don't have it," Resi shouted back. "I'd sure like it myself, though..."

Their standoff ensued for several unbearable minutes. What was worse for Resi was the malfunction symbol flashing on the Zyler-9's LED screen. His weapon was kaput. The trigger mechanism had even locked up in protest. Yet he knew Jeffrins had to be suitably impressed by the instant fragmentation of his associates and was keeping his distance. It was an eerie interval in the history of their lives. They taunted one another and talked trash with Laira's fountainhead between them, her amplified spirit still dancing obliviously on while the sizzling crystal stream replenished it.

Sam Jeffrins was always an impatient man. If he could not immediately get what was wanted he always forced the issue. With stealthy movements, somehow he had moved around the fountainhead to a closer proximity with his desired target. He had the back of Resi's head partially in range. His crouching figure stepped up to get a better kill shot, but he slipped and fell silently into Laira McKinney's neon fountainhead, disappearing completely into the crystalline lava. Still Laira's spirit danced on, and Carlton Resi made a mental note that her apparition was not an illusion.

# Chapter 12

# Of Fire and Water

It was a torrential beating of wings nearly deafening him that drove Resi into a fast heartbeat of panic. He'd sequestered himself as best he could inside some nearby scattered electronic equipment whose tarp he now crouched beneath. Overhead the whooshing sound continued as the last of the Tomu creatures flew out from the hybrid trees toward the tunnel.

Rooksana Zu was nowhere to be seen, he'd searched much of the underground labyrinth while he was able. An ensuing pandemonium around him made Resi take cover several times, especially when small explosions occurred with the hissing pop of electric wires on fire. An acrid smoke was slowly lining the ceiling of this vast arboretum and electronic wonderland and he knew he must escape it without further delay. Around him human body parts in a gruesome carnival of color horrifically festooned the now crimson lab center.

When Resi was able to find an exit door it took most of his strength to bash it open with a metal rod and make his escape. Coughing and spitting out soot, he found himself outside and back near the cliff-side they had arrived at hours earlier. The sky was lit with explosions and the sight of multitudinous Tomu creatures flying off for the city. Many of them were atop the glistening mucous mounds with their festering flies that he and Zu had already had the misfortune of meeting. The creatures he saw appeared to be fueling themselves from the phallic-shaped pillar mounds before rejoining those already in flight. It was an eerie sight that Carlton Resi would never forget. He was relieved to find his Cypress phone still wedged in a pocket of his now torn and singed canvas jacket. Hurriedly he began taking non-stop pictures of the spectacle, which became remarkably well-lit due to the intermittently illuminated sky created by a plethora of crisscrossing laser lights and those of circling helicopters. The endless night had banished the sun from bringing dawn.

The frenzy befalling Amsterdam and its surrounding areas was one of destructive fury comparable to a natural disaster. Fortified with their toxic mucous and more, the flying Tomu creatures virulently attacked the city and its early morning population, creating a pattern of destructiveness lethal to its core. Cars, bicyclists, trams, and pedestrians alike were assaulted and chewed to simmering bits by the Tomu aliens, whose fangs and strong wings left a trail of disemboweled pulp in their wake. Emergency sirens sounded everywhere, including the surprising retorts of outlawed and very ineffective firearms.

The Amsterdam canals were filled with a flotsam of floating human remains as the attack continued. The once murky water turned into a variety of unpleasant hues, some of which were simply rust red with spilled blood. People leaped to their deaths from many tall buildings at the city's center as helicopters crashed around them. The train station suddenly became a scene of mayhem and devastation as the alien creatures descended on moving trains and overturned them. The shrill cries of countless victims became a grim chorus for the unfolding event gaining a pernicious momentum with each bloodletting second. Plus many boats – large and small, of every nautical description – were submerged and fragmented with unimaginable rending sounds, as the Tomu creatures remorselessly overwhelmed and sank them, killing all life aboard them.

Looking out the windows of his gabled and historic canal front home, the Magister gasped at what he saw and, dropping his cane unawares, nearly collapsed onto the floor. Instantly he knew it had to be the outcome of the Maze Niner experience, and – hastily putting on his bifocals – kept muttering, "No, Hiram, no," as he began accessing his phone, which already had a lengthy list of missed calls from associates and civic leaders.

Immediately he called Velmer Ebos and was informed of the updated status of the unspeakable event, too unreal at first for any rational explanation.

"All hell has broken out, Magister," Ebos informed him. "What are they? They're huge things resembling flying apes of some kind, just destroying everything and everyone in their path! The police and military units aren't doing well out there – the city is in shambles…All traffic has ground to a halt and people are being killed everywhere."

"I'd swear you were out of your mind, if I now didn't feel out of my own," the Magister said. "What about our weapons cache? Can we fight them —?"

"We only have a couple of Zyler-9's left…I don't know what their energy capacities are at present, or how long they'd last. It's an experimental weapon we've never mass manufactured for sale to the military."

"Blame it on goddamn politics," the Magister said. "But who could foresee such a catastrophe? The return of these Tomu things…!"

"Is that what they are, sir, similar to whatever was here during the Alien War?"

"Rather a transmogrified version of what once was here, Velmer, and confined to the countryside. Now my deranged partner, de Hazeraux, has somehow created a more bestial version from what once was simply toxic mold plants, I would venture…and has, alas, succeeded."

"I've already handed out small firearms to the men around every square inch of your property, sir," Ebos said. On his desk there were four CCTV monitors showing the Magister the frantic barricading of his property with sandbags and other improvised devices. Fires everywhere burned out of control. The activity was indeed frenetic, but they needed more men and materials. Every vehicle mustered into service helped form a line of defense, Ebos declared, if they just had the wherewithal to achieve it.

The Magister then instructed Ebos to do whatever was necessary to safeguard his canal house and more importantly the conclave itself, where most of his factory assets were. He didn't have time to finish. One of the airborne creatures had alighted with a loud thump on the ledge outside his window sill, its shimmering jade wings slowly folding back onto its moldy body, while its face – he could swear it! – morphed into a grotesque replica of Adolph Hitler's own.

He had only a brief moment to recognize it, for in the next second the beast emerged through the splintering window – and crushed the Magister's screaming form before devouring his head with a quick, crunching sound.

"Magister?" the worried voice of Velmer Ebos could be heard asking through the dropped cell phone. "Are you all right?"

Concurrently in the red-light district nearby, similar beheadings of naked prostitutes still at work took place in a seeming blur. Their disemboweled and blood-splashed bodies were unceremoniously dumped into the canals by the ravenous Tomu attackers. One had its sanguine jaws around a nude couple, whose copulation was interrupted by its huge fangs breaking them in half. All manner of small buildings and shops were reduced to rubble by the Tomu's wings battering down anything within their vicinity.

Inexorably the maritime city burned. It burned as if firebombed from a world war bombardment, long thought buried in the annals of forgotten history by whoever wrote its twisted truth.

Rooksana Zu walked, crept, and stealthily climbed to the cliff-side promontory where, according to Hiram de Hazeraux's instructions, the alien Tomu craft would descend from the heavens to take her. At that moment the heavens were garishly bright with the fires burning Amsterdam and the overhead flight patterns of NATO fighter jets, firing missiles at the airborne

Tomu invaders. The warring noises sent shock waves into Zu as each missile found its target and destroyed several Tomu creatures. They were blown into spinning hordes of an unrecognizable pulpy mass Rooksana feared might fall onto her. But she knew enough of them still were alive.

In each hand she held a SPLANX tablet and waited, watching an endless stream of encrypted codes flash by on the electronic screens – knowing, perhaps, the codes were an ongoing interactive program processing between the tablets and the approaching Tomu spacecraft. A type of digital synchronizing was taking place, no doubt technically aligning both tablets into a harmonious mode lacking before. All it took was a simple understanding of the mumbo-jumbo that de Hazeraux's technology amounted to, and somehow she was able to conjure up its latent potential, thanks to her study of its maker's blueprint.

Still she wondered if what was supposed to happen was remotely possible. She knew Carlton Resi was probably dead, and – if not – could never easily find her now. Upon reaching the promontory she had thrown away the last vestige of a cell phone, still clutching her backpack as if it held secrets to her survival in another cosmic realm.

With high-powered mini-cam binoculars she began to record and study parts of the sky while waiting. Eventually she saw the approaching Tomu craft, glowing like a small comet. It had a remarkable blue, oblong shape and was super fast in darting through the debris in this section of the earth's atmosphere. Seeing it she thought of Jane Dawson and her mother as well, wondering what they would think upon seeing it as she now did. Was it possible the craft would land and remove components from de Hazeraux's lab? It might be too late, she knew, for all that was left down there was sabotaged by her, including whatever allowed de Hazeraux to conjure forth her sister's 'spirit' in all its gargantuan majesty, something she had nonetheless paid homage to before doing what she had to do.

Supposing too, her great-grandmother were somehow aboard that craft, even as a spiritual entity stabilized by Tomu science...Would Rooksana be able to deal with it, this hybrid transformation of her kin into what the aliens needed to survive here – and what they surely needed from her?

As she wondered she wept as well and held each tablet high up, as if in offering to the arriving Tomu visitors. Codes continued to race across her mind, as they did on the blue, glowing, SPLANX screens. Her lips moved tremulously as the whining oscillation began to vibrate throughout her body, preparing it for the ineluctable reception to come. It was a digital annunciation of sorts, something she felt and heard now in all its terrible power and glory! When and if she succumbed to it, Rooksana Zu would be both dead and alive forever – and forever would she be able to serve the Tomu race of hybrid beings.

A few of the darting, NATO fighter jets, disintegrated instantly within the brilliant aura of the approaching Tomu craft. Swirling wind almost propelled her off the rocky promontory, yet Rooksana continued staring straight up with the SPLANX tablets upraised in both hands. The oscillating tension within her was unbearable and she knew she couldn't keep it up much longer. One long, yellow beam of laser-light began to suffuse her form into its funnel shape. She was being taken! The craft descended steadily coming closer. Opening her eyes, she was able to see through the blinding ray what was vividly emblazoned on the approaching craft's wings: the twin swastika symbols of the Third Reich with their clockwise arms unmistakably larger than life.

With a scream Rooksana brought each tablet crashing against the other with all her might. For a nano-second all matter parted before her and the ensuing explosion decimating her and the craft above could be heard for miles, so massive and nuclear-splitting did it prove to be. A huge tongue of fire engulfed the cliff-side, torching it into a sulfurous heat wall, stretching for endless miles.

Everywhere the still flying Tomu creatures ignited like fireworks above the North Sea then fell into it. In Amsterdam's centrum the marauding creatures stopped, as if the air had been let out of them and fell dead as Dutch doorknockers to the ground. Some of the dying monsters plummeted with fiery wings into the canals, emitting cacophonous squeals as they sizzled.

All of them were dead almost instantaneously and what remained of these fallen hybrid bodies were now heaped everywhere throughout the city for the emergency trucks and military units to clean up.

It was the greatest bio-hazard clean up ever, one local newspaper would proclaim later on its front page.

"So much for the Vitruvian Man of Leonardo da Vinci," Carlton Resi said, sipping the tea, Myri, the ex-prostitute offered him in her apartment nearby Canal Street. Her left arm was still in a cast from the day of the Tomu invasion but the rest of her was remarkably intact – and attractive.

"How do you mean?"

"Well, Hiram de Hazeraux was a devotee of Leonardo's, but his hybrid experiments with Tomu beings led him astray. What he created turned the human body away from its being an analogy for the harmonious workings of the universe..."

"Into something decidedly the opposite," Myri agreed. "Well, I'm just glad you made it out all right, Resi. I was worried to say the least."

"I made it out, yeah, but I guess the Magister didn't. What about the Dawson sisters?"

"I haven't a clue as to where they're at. They have apparently disappeared. Remember their little book shop?"

"I do indeed."

"It was burned out during the night of the Tomu invasion.

Nothing remains of it."

Thoughtfully Resi stroked his bandaged chin and shook his head.

That's unfortunate, isn't it? So much for them and the dream of Eco-Conservancy...

"Do you think Amsterdam will ever recover?"

"It will," said Myri, pouring him more tea. "After all, the whole world is helping us. For once the Dutch government has enough money to start doing things again." She smiled up at Resi. "I just admire you so much now, Resi, what you did and all, in tracking the ghost of Laira McKinney to where it led you."

"Yeah, but I had no idea it would lead to all this." He glanced through her muslin curtained window at the reconstruction crews working outside. "Nor did Laira, maybe..."

"You saw her again, didn't you?"

"Well, sure, after it was all over. Not just her blown-up simulacrum in Hiram's underground kingdom. But after Rooksana lit up everything for good and the creatures fell."

"And when the Tomu space craft exploded..."

"Yeah, and somehow I made it from the cliff, running for all I was worth. I fell down, exhausted, and must have passed out. I don't know if it was an hour or a second later when I came to, but I saw her then, as I will always remember her, in a colorful summer dress and bonnet."

"It was after all her apparition, and you didn't need your equipment to see her."

"Of course not, it was her full-bodied apparition drifting towards me, floating just above the scorched earth really. Smiling like she always did, but I was scared. For the first time ever I was scared seeing her ghost. I stood up and she nodded, then passed right through me and disappeared."

"Wow."

"Uh-huh. And I felt, well, like healed. The pain from all the days and the nights before just disappeared like she did."

"That's incredible."

"It is," said Resi, lighting a cigarette, still in a contemplative mode. "I'll wonder about it all till I'm an old man, I'm sure. I've tried to understand the power of the SPLANX tablet, as Rooksana Zu probably did. 'When the natures of our power and all power are joined to and catalyzed by the SPLANX transformation, either heaven or hell results...' That's how she put it. She told me that de Hazeraux left her strange clues for her to understand what SPLANX was about – and finally how to use it, of course. SPLANX transforms what the eye receives into a digital 'soul' of sorts, which paranormal energy sustains and is sustained by. It becomes a conduit through an unreal 'nature's window' in order to reach the supernatural, and of course the Nazis wanted it desperately way back when. Whoever controls the SPLANX becomes a superman, of course, and they let Hiram continue to develop if for them."

"The Nazi descendants, you mean?"

"Whoever was in that otherworldly craft Rooksana destroyed...They were hybrid humans working hand-in-hand with the Tomu aliens. Each had become the other in order to survive and we probably couldn't tell which is which if we had to. But Hiram de Hazeraux could, and he found a way to contact their nexus of leaders – and also to develop the 'real' monsters invading us, cloned from the dead DNA of the Tomu plant molds, creating something at the evolutionary apex of his research and experiments."

"He fused the spiritual with — "

"With the somatic DNA of Tomu beings, which were originally plant-like, and their evolved beings worked on fusing human DNA with their own. He did what the Nazi scientists were working on in the middle 20th century, during World War II."

"That's, uh, really incredible, Resi."

"I know. He devised beings both simultaneously dead and yet

alive, all via SPLANX and its activating power. Their intelligence was in that spaceship that blew up, but I don't think their bodies were. Only their paranormal intelligence guided that craft, like it was on auto-pilot, from another galaxy and planet, perhaps."

Myri stubbed out her own cigarette, shaking her head, dwelling on all this like it were a new version of the Kennedy assassination.

"You should write about all this, Resi, like Rooksana, the occult reporter would have."

"Something tells me I better not. The world saw an extraterrestrial invasion in the flesh, not ghosts made real. The world has to believe in what is physically tangible, not the stuff of dreams, belonging to a madman, genius, or saint."

Resi took out his cell phone, preparing to call his Los Angeles office to let them know he was all right and to not believe the internet reports of his demise.

"You know, Resi," said Myri, "I know you like the pickled herring of Amsterdam. When I was once angry at you, really pissed, I hoped you'd gag eating one."

Resi paused before leaving the apartment.

"Well, you know, as long as it's not a real red herring, Myri," he said, and with a smile he opened the door and left.

**COSMIC
EGG
BOOKS**

If you prefer to spend your nights with Vampires and
Werewolves rather than the mundane then we publish the books
for you. If your preference is for Dragons and Faeries or Angels
and Demons – we should be your first stop. Perhaps your
perfect partner has artificial skin or comes from another planet –
step right this way. Our curiosity shop contains treasures you
will enjoy unearthing. If your passion is Fantasy (including
magical realism and spiritual fantasy), Horror or Science Fiction
(including Steampunk), Cosmic Egg books will
feed your hunger.